Old Acquaintances
Gayle Buck

Also by Gayle Buck

Tempting Sarah
The Waltzing Widow
The Holybrooke Curse
Season of Joy
Hearts Betrayed
Chistmas Cheer
Old Acquaintances
Mutual Consent
The Chester Charade
The Desperate Viscount
Lady Althea's Bargain
Fredericka's Folly
Love for Lucinda
Lord Darlington's Darling
The Demon Rake
Lord Rathbone's Flirt
Miss Dower's Paragon
Belle's Beau
Cassandra's Deception
Love's Masquerade
The Righteous Rakehell
A Magnificent Match
The Hidden Heart
Willowswood Match
A Chance Encounter

The Fleeing Heiress
Lady Cecily's Scheme
Cupid's Choice
Lord John's Lady
Honor Besieged

Chapter One

The well-sprung carriage rocked in a soothing rhythm. She was perfectly comfortable. She had a brick to her warm her feet and a heavy lap rug tucked snugly over her legs. In her hands, she held a favorite book. And she was returning home to Elmswood Hall for the remainder of the yuletide holidays. She should have been content.

But Miss Judith Grantham was restive. She finally admitted it to herself when her eyes drifted away from the page of her book for the hundredth time since starting on her journey. Not one to fling herself after a lost cause, Judith put aside the book and gave herself over to the changing landscape outside the glazed window.

Snowflakes flashed past the glass, winking in the late afternoon sunlight like so many bits of shiny tinsel. The white fields and hedgerows were marked by tall pristine drifts. It was an enchanting prospect, but Miss Grantham was not in the least appreciative.

She sighed, wondering what had gotten into her. She should be anticipating getting home to Elmswood, but instead her spirits sank ever lower as the carriage closed the distance to her destination.

She knew the reason, of course. It was the same at the end of every visit to her sister's sprawling home, when she swore, amid the loud protests of her nieces and nephews, that she would be glad of the peace at Elmswood. But the truth was that she missed the companionship and confidences of her sister, her brother-in-law's quiet wit, and the numerous progeny who dragged on her hands, demanding her attention, and who generally besieged one whom they called the best of aunts.

Judith knew herself to be fortunate. She enjoyed the adoration of her sister's family and was a welcome and frequent visitor. She was the possessor of a fair estate, unentailed and bequeathed by her mother upon her birth, with the added benefit of an adequate income that had been settled on her through the terms of her father's will.

Though she hardly gave a thought to it, she knew that she was considered to be a young woman of uncommon good looks. She was of a willowy height that lent grace and proportion of a deep bosom and curved hips. Her eyes were dark smoke gray that could lighten either with amusement or anger. Her hair was dark and curling, her winged brows well-marked, her nose straight, and her mouth delectably full. In fact, there was but one flaw attached to Miss Judith Grantham and that had to do with her past.

When Miss Grantham had been brought out for her first Season, she had become an instant success. The gentlemen raved in admiration of the "English Tea Rose," as she was immediately dubbed, and though there were ladies who experienced twinges of envy, little was said against Miss Grantham because her kindness of manner quickly won over even some of the haughtiest of dames.

Miss Grantham had therefore enjoyed exceptional popularity. When her engagement to Sir Peregrine Ashford was announced, it was touted as a very satisfactory ending to a spectacular career, for Sir Peregrine was himself as popular with the gentlemen as he was with the ladies.

But that had been five years ago, before Judith had jilted Sir Peregrine, for reasons still unknown beyond the parties involved, and she had earned for herself a reputation. At four-and-twenty, Miss Grantham was still considered a beauty but quite beyond the marriageable age. She might still have been seriously courted if there had been a gentleman audacious enough to brave both Miss Grantham's reputation and the aura of mystery that had clung to her. For there always seemed to lurk a faint hint of amusement in her eyes, as though she viewed the world from a vantage point not given to others. The distance in her gaze put off even the most obtuse of gentlemen, who uncomfortably suspected that they were the object of Miss Grantham's amusement. So Miss Grantham was looked upon as an unattainable beauty; certainly worthy of admiration but never to be approached.

Judith was well aware of what was said of her and it amused her to encourage the speculation because for the most part the life she led perfectly suited her. It was only in rare moments such as this, when she had left the warmth and cheer of her sister's home, that she was not quite content with her lot. After the bustle, Elmswood seemed particularly echoing during the remainder of the Christmas holidays, but Judith always made a point of returning to Elmswood so that she could uphold her role on Boxing Day, the first week-day after Christmas, when by tradition she handed out a Christmas gift box to each member of her household.

Of course, it was pleasant to be mistress of her own household and her staff did decorate Elsmwood in the traditional manner with holly and fir, and roaring fires provided welcoming heat in every room. But it was not as though she would be sharing the warmth with anyone else, she thought with a touch of melancholy.

Judith realized that she was fast sinking into a maudlin self-pity and she gave herself a thorough mental shaking. She detested self-pity in others and it appalled her that she could come close to indulging in it herself. "Enough of that, my girl," she said firmly. She could have had that other well enough, but she had chosen against it. Actually, she had no true regrets for her decision. It had been the right one at the time. But once in a while the thought crept up on her to wonder what her life might have been if she had married.

For the briefest of moments her thoughts touched on Sir Peregrine Ashford. After she had jilted him, it had been a very long time before she had been able to think of him without feeling a constriction in her throat. But in five years Judith had learned that time had a way of softening certain memories and she no longer felt that flash of pain.

Sir Peregrine had been the most attractive gentleman she had ever known. As surrounded as she had been by gentlemen, she had still been attracted to Sir Peregrine upon first sighting his broad shoulders and the crisp curling hair that touched his collar. When he had turned his head and his incredible piercing blue eyes met hers, Judith had literally felt her heart take flight.

A reminiscent smile played about her mouth and her eyes held a certain light. She and Sir Peregrine had been quite a match, complimenting one another in every way. Except one, Judith remembered. Her smile faded a little as her thoughts carried her into the past. It had been an unfortunate happening, but certainly her eyes had been irrevocably opened to the truth. And she had never been one to shirk the truth once it was borne in upon her.

The carriage slowed, distracting Judith from her somber thoughts. She leaned closer to the window and realized that the vehicle was actually stopping. Judith unlatched the window and put out her head. "Edward, why have we stopped?" she called out. The cold frosted her breath.

The driver was climbing down from the box, having snubbed his reins. "A mail coach has overturned and the road is blocked, miss. It looks to be a bad accident."

Judith snapped shut the window. She did not wait for the carriage door to be opened, but unlatched it herself and stepped down. Snow crunched under her boots. She felt the immediate impact of the icy air against her face, but fortunately she was attired in a warm pelisse and a heavy traveling dress and the cold did not penetrate to any great degree.

"Miss, ye'll catch your death," objected Edward.

"Nonsense, I shall do no such thing," said Judith firmly. Nevertheless, she was glad of her muff and thrust her hands deeper into its warmth. "I wish to see for myself the damage and whether anyone has been hurt." The coachman was long inured to his mistress's firmness of purpose and without further protest he helpfully placed a hand under her elbow when it appeared that she might slip on a particularly bad patch of ice as they walked around to the front of the team of horses.

Judith was appalled at the sight that met her eyes. The mail coach was on its side in a drift, baggage had been flung in every direction, and the frightened horses were tangled in the traces. The passengers were seated on whatever was at hand, or standing in the snow, depending upon their inclinations. Most appeared simply bruised and shaken, but here and there was the unmistakable show of blood. "My word," said Judith inadequately.

"I'll just go help the coachman untangle his cattle, miss."

"Of course, Edward, pray do whatever you can," said Judith. She looked about again at the passengers, some of whom appeared to be haranguing a lanky young gentleman who was sunk down on a portmanteau and holding his head in his heads. It was clear from the shrill accusations that the young gentleman had been the one at fault for the accident, having taken over the driver's whip and setting the mail coach at a dangerous pace over the frozen road.

Dismissing those vigorously scolding individuals as probably undesirous of her help, Judith approached a woeful-looking gentleman who held a handkerchief to his brow. "Sir, I see that you are injured. Is there something that I might do?" she asked.

The gentleman grimaced as he glanced up at her. "A bit of flying glass, it was. I thank you kindly, my lady, but it is naught more than a scratch. Perhaps you might see to the young lady there, who I suspicion was quite shook up. She ended on the bottom when we was all thrown about."

Judith looked around, surprised. She had not before noticed the young woman who stood somewhat separated from the others, perhaps because a light flurry of snow had blurred the outline of her pale gray pelisse. But now that Judith's attention had been drawn to her, she could discern the weary droop in the slight figure.

Judith went over immediately. "My dear ma'am, may I be of assistance? Have you been hurt?"

The young woman lifted her head and Judith was struck at once by the budding loveliness of her heart-shaped countenance. Judith's compassion was fully aroused by the paper white of the girl's face and the pathetic look in her black-fringed china-blue eyes. The schoolgirl – for of such an age she judged her to be – had wrapped her arms about herself and it was plain that she was freezing cold.

Judith held out her gloved hand. "Come with me at once. You must not stay out in this weather. You are not dressed for it."

The girl automatically took Judith's hand but she held back, objecting faintly. "My-my portmanteau and-and bandbox. What shall I do?"

"I shall have my coachman gather them up for you. Are these the ones?" asked Judith, pointing at the meager baggage at the girl's feet. At her nod, Judith called out to her servant, who was returning from helping the mail coach's driver. "Edward, pray put these up. I shall be taking this young lady to the next posting house."

"Aye, miss. And I have promised to take word of the accident, so it would be best if we was to get on, Miss Judith."

Judith nodded. "Very well. Come, child, let us climb up into the carriage. You shall be warmer in a trice, I promise you." With that, she led her unexpected guest to her carriage and opened the door for her. The girl climbed in somewhat stiffly and Judith followed, closing the door behind her. She sat down and turned her head to smile at the girl, who had sunk down on the seat with almost an air of dejection.

Judith took note of the girl's expression but did not comment on it. Instead, she said bracingly, "I was just wishing for company. We shall share the lap rug. There you are, tucked in as snug as you please. You must take my muff, for I at least have gloves. And there is a brick to our feet. What more could one wish for?"

The girl burst into tears.

Chapter Two

Judith was taken aback. "My dear! What have I said? I certainly never meant to offend you."

"No, no! You have been so kind – so good!" stammered the girl, tears slipping swiftly down her cheeks. She opened her reticule and frantically searched in it, at last bringing out a small handkerchief. She made an obvious effort to choke back her tears. She blew her nose, which Judith noticed with a touch of envy was not pinkened in the slightest by the violent exercise.

Judith reached out and captured one of the girl's agitated hands. Even through her glove she could feel that the slender fingers were chilled. "Child, you are safe with me. I am Miss Judith Grantham of Elmswood Hall. It is easily seen that you are out of water. Whatever possessed you to travel by mail coach? I am persuaded that your family never countenanced it," she said gently.

The girl threw a scared glance at her. "I do not know what you mean. I frequently travel by mail coach. It-it is perfectly comfortable for one of my station."

Judith put up her brows. There was the merest hint of a smile in her eyes. "And what is your station, miss?"

The girl threw up her chin and challenged the older woman with a bold stare. "Why, I am a lady's maid, to be sure."

Judith could not help but laugh. She pressed the girl's fingers before releasing her hand. "Dear girl, a lady's maid is never so young, nor so pretty, as you are. Nor would one be attired in such an elegantly cut pelisse. And pray do not tell me it is your mistress's cast-off, for I shall not believe you. Your manner and your attire both proclaim you to be gently born, so you must not attempt to pull the wool over my eyes, if you please."

The girl cast a glance down at her gray pelisse and, apparently realizing that it was futile to deny the truth of Miss Grantham's observation, she sighed. Her china-blue eyes bravely met Judith's gaze. "Since you have found me out, I shall not try to hoodwink you, ma'am. I am running away from my guardian, who is a detestable beast. And though I do appreciate your kindness in carrying me to the next posting house, I hope that you do not feel compelled to persuade me to change my mind. I am quite determined never to return to my cousin's domination."

Judith was silent a moment. "I see. Pray, what is your name?"

The girl hesitated briefly and then she shrugged. "I doubt that it signifies, for I shall not see you again. I am Cecily Brown. I hope that you are not too offended that I do not divulge my direction as well, but you must see that simply would not do."

The name meant nothing to Judith and she was disappointed. If by remote chance she had heard of the girl's family, as a family acquaintance she might have been able to offer the hospitality of Elmswood Hall and perhaps provided a neutral ground upon which the girl and her guardian could thrash out their differences. As it was, she knew that she could do little but offer the girl some food for thought.

"Cecily, have you perfectly thought out what you are attempting? I know nothing of your circumstances, but surely your guardian would not wish you to disappear without some assurance of your continued well-being. And pray, how do you intend to live? Do you have relatives or friends who would be willing to take you in?"

Cecily shook her head. "I have no one but my cousin. And as for him, I think that he will be heartily glad that I am gone. He never wished to have me cast on him, you see, and that is why he came up with his horrid notion to marry me to the first gentleman that he found acceptable." Her bosom rose as deep indignation overcame her. "Miss Grantham, the gentleman is twice my age and he is bald and he smokes a cigar, which I cannot at all abide! I shall not marry him, I shall not!"

There was a hint of hysteria in her voice that Judith was quick to note. "The gentleman in question is not clamoring for your hand at this moment, so you may rest easy for a while yet," she said with deliberate callousness.

After a stunned moment, Cecily unwillingly laughed. "I am sorry, Miss Grantham! I never meant to treat you to a turn of drama. Only it is all so idiotic. Why, I have not even been brought out. I think it frightfully unfair of Per-of my cousin. I should so like to go to London." She ended on such a wistful note that it touched the older woman's heart.

Judith shook her head. It would not do to become too sympathetic. Cecily's story struck such chords of understanding within her and it was an effort to recall that there was another side. The overbearing guardian may have had his reasons. There, it is plain whose side I have aligned myself with, thought Judith with exasperation. Overbearing, indeed! And he very likely wears a corset and helps himself too liberally to snuff, she thought whimsically. Aloud, she said, "Cecily, in all conscience I must ask you to reconsider your ill-considered flight. I would feel responsible if something untoward should happen to you once I have set you down."

"I appreciate your sentiments, Miss Grantham. But truly, I am quite capable of caring for myself. I have had the splendid notion to enter service, you see, and so I shall do very well," said Cecily with bright confidence, her beautiful eyes shining from beneath the longest black lashes that Judith had ever seen on a female.

"Oh, my dear," she said helplessly, her gaze traveling from Cecily's lovely fresh face to her slender figure and back again. She took a breath. "I am sorry to inform you of it, Cecily, but no one is likely to hire anyone quite as pretty as you are. Except perhaps just the sort of gentleman that you are so adamant against marrying. And I fear that it will not be the gentleman's cigar smoke that you would find particularly objectionable, but his attempts to-to steal a kiss." She felt herself entirely inadequate at relaying the realities of the world to a young girl such as Cecily and she waited somewhat uncomfortably for her companion's inevitable query for enlightenment.

But Cecily's expression was not one of confusion. She looked surprised, then thoughtful. "Once, as a small child, I surprised Papa with one of the maids. I suppose that is the sort of thing you mean. No, I should not care for that. Perhaps I shall become a mantua maker instead."

Judith was taken aback. "Cecily, do I perfectly understand what you are saying about your father?"

"Oh, yes. Before Papa died, he was a bit of a rake. And though I do not know precisely, I suppose it meant he was quite fond of maids," said Cecily with an innocent and inquiring glance.

Judith sat back against the seat, her breath quite knocked out of her. "Indeed, I suppose so," she said weakly, clearing her throat. When Cecily turned her head away to glance out of the carriage window, where the day could be seen as fast-growing dim, Judith studied her profile with a mixture of astonishment and bewildered estimation. She was fast coming to realize that Cecily Brown was not an ordinary miss. Cecily presented the appearance of a schoolgirl, naïve and trusting, and yet Judith had seen depths of character and experience that belonged to someone several years older.

Her determination not to fall in with her guardian's wishes was perhaps nothing much out of the common way, but coupled as it was to her ability to act upon her decisions made Cecily unusual indeed, thought Judith, remembering a young girl who had not had the same courage of her convictions. As for Cecily's casual reference to her father's peccadillo and her acceptance of it, Judith thought she was never more shocked in her life. She herself had known nothing of the opposite sex until her engagement. Her cheeks flushed warmly at her unbidden memories and she hastily returned her thoughts to Cecily.

Despite herself and knowing that she should not become involved more than she already was, Judith turned over in her mind what Cecily had said of her situation. There had to be something she could do to aid the girl in establishing herself happily. Judith felt that she must make some sort of effort in Cecily's behalf, or she would always wonder what had happened to the girl.

The carriage slowed and stopped. Judith put down the window as her coachman came up to it. Snow swirled briefly with a gust of cold wind. "What is toward, Edward?" she asked.

"We have come to the posting house, miss," said the coachman. He threw a look at the dusk sky. "I mislike the weather, Miss Judith. The wind is sharpening a bit and the snow is heavier."

Judith made a quick decision. "I shall step down with Miss Brown for a quick cup of tea while you report the accident to the innkeeper, Edward. Then we shall go on as quickly as possible to reach Elmswood before nightfall."

She and Cecily walked into the inn. The innkeeper's wife recognized Judith and she expressed surprise to see her. "Miss Grantham, it is a pleasure, I am sure. It is that rare that you honor us with your company, what with Elmswood so close and all. What may I do for you?"

Judith looked about the coffee room, which was nearly deserted at that hour, and decided against bespeaking a private parlor. "I think that we shall have a strong cup of tea, and perhaps a light repast for my young friend."

Cecily looked alarmed. "Really, I do not wish supper. I feel as though I could not swallow a bite. It is rather warm in here, is it not?"

Judith stared at her, frowning. The coffee room was warmed by the fire in the grate, but it was not so warm that Cecily should become flushed by the heat. She hoped the girl was not becoming ill. "We shall have just the tea, then."

"Certainly, miss. It is shaping up to be a bad storm tonight. I know that you ladies will be wishful to get on to Elmswood, so I will bring the tea straight away," said the innkeeper's wife.

"Oh, but I shall not be going with Miss Grantham. I wish to bespeak a room for the night so that I may catch the mail coach in the morning," said Cecily.

The innkeeper's wife looked at her in dismay. "I am sorry, miss, but we haven't a room to spare. What with the weather and all, we've had more than our share of travelers who have decided to stay until first light. If you was a gentleman, I might see if there was someone who would not mind sharing his room with a stranger. But as it is, I haven't even a closet for a decent young lady."

Cecily stared at the woman, speechless. She did not seem to know what to do. Judith took matters into her own hands. "My dear child, you must certainly come home with me."

"But I cannot impose on you further, Miss Grantham. You have already been so kind," said Cecily.

"Nonsense. It will be you who will be doing me the favor. Elmswood is very quiet this Christmas. Indeed, I would not mind it in the least if half a dozen more personages chose to become marooned on my doorstep. It would make for quite a jolly little party, don't you think?" asked Judith in a reassuring way. Cecily responded to Judith's jest, though her smile wavered a little.

The innkeeper's wife saw that the matter was settled and she nodded in satisfaction. She bustled off at once for the promised tea and she was soon back, saying that she always kept a hot pot handy. Judith declined sugar but accepted milk for her tea. She saw that Cecily was fond of a very sweetened tea and it almost made her teeth hurt to watch the girl sip at the resulting syrup.

Before the ladies had quite finished their cups of tea, Edward the coachman came up to inform Judith that the innkeeper had promised to send out help to the stranded mail coach passengers. "The snow is becoming that heavy, miss, that I think it best that we get on as quick as we can," he said, casting an anxious glance at his mistress's cup.

"We shall go at once. Miss Brown will be accompanying us after all, Edward. I hope that you have not set down her baggage," said Judith, rising from the table. Cecily immediately leaped up, not wishing to delay their departure and thus be any more of a burden on her benefactress.

"No, miss. That is to say, I will put it back in the carriage this instant," said Edward.

Judith nodded and walked out of the coffee room to find the innkeeper's wife so that she could pay the bill. With the woman's good wishes ringing on the air, the carriage bound for Elmswood once more turned onto the icy road. Snow swirled about its dark moving shape, then it was gone into the dusk.

Chapter Three

The welcoming light and warmth of Elmswood Hall were all that Judith had hoped. The scent of fir and pine and warm wax wafted out the open door, drawing the travelers inside.

Judith was glad to step into the hall and hear the butler's welcome. "I am happy to be home, Withers. This young lady is Miss Cecily Brown. The coach she was on had an unfortunate accident and so I have offered the hospitality of Elmswood to her. Pray see that a room is prepared for her," she said, beginning to draw off her gloves.

"At once, Miss Grantham," said Withers, motioning for a footman to take up the portmanteau and bandbox that had been brought in from the carriage. "I took the liberty of setting up a cold collation in the drawing room in anticipation of your arrival and I shall bring in tea in a quarter hour."

"Bless you, Withers. That will be just time enough to change from this damp travel dress," said Judith, bestowing a grateful smile on him. She turned to Cecily and took her hands in her own. Again, she noticed how cold the girl's slender fingers were. "The footman will show you the way to your room. I shall meet with you again in the drawing room for supper in a few minutes."

Cecily smiled her acquiescence and then followed the footman carrying her baggage up the stairway that occupied one side of the entry hall. Her weariness was underscored by the droop of her slim shoulders. She was in no mind to demur at whatever was proposed, only wishing for rest. Through the fog that had settled over her, she noticed the festive loops of holly and fir that decorated the graceful lift of stairs.

Her wavering spirits were comforted by the cheery sight. She was safe here, she thought gratefully, and stifled a yawn.

Judith watched her guest ascend, a tiny frown between her winged brows. She pulled her gloves through her fingers without being conscious of it.

The butler was thoroughly familiar with Miss Grantham's moods and he observed this sign of perturbation with interest. He wondered what there was about Miss Brown that should prove disquieting to Miss Grantham. "Miss Grantham, will there be anything else?" he asked quietly.

Judith was startled out of her thoughts. "No, not at the moment, Withers," she said. She walked to the stairs and swiftly went up them and thence to her bedroom. Her maid, who she had sent off earlier in a separate carriage with all of her baggage, had arrived some time before her and was waiting to help her out of the heavy travel dress. In moments, Judith was freshly attired in a long-sleeved merino gown of a soft dove gray that enhanced the smoky shade of her eyes. Her hair, freed at last of the confines of her bonnet, had been brushed into soft waves.

Judith went downstairs, thinking to join Cecily. Instead, she discovered a small group of strangers who were loosely clustered about her butler in the entry hall and besieging him with loud statements. Judith paused on the last step, her hand resting on the banister, surprised.

The woman in the group spied Judith and surged forward. "You must be Miss Grantham, then. I was just telling this fudsy-faced butler of yours that you had left word at the posting house that any who could not find a bed there would be welcome at Elmswood Hall," she said firmly.

Withers rolled his eyes in appeal as one of the gentlemen asserted that what the woman had said was so. Judith was entirely taken aback and for a long second she was speechless. Though she was unaware of it, her very immobility and the exquisite austerity of her dress lent her an air of command. The woman dropped back a pace and the others quieted, waiting.

Judith realized that she was the object of all eyes. She focused on the woman in front of her. "Who might you be, ma'am?" she asked quietly, trying to make sense of the happening.

The woman flushed, thinking that she was being gently reprimanded for her own curt greeting. "I am Mrs. Nickleby, and that gentleman is Mr. Nickleby. We were on our way to our son's house when the mail coach was overturned by his young lordship, who, as I made certain to tell him, should have known better when anyone could tell he was tipsy as a wheelbarrow."

"Aye, his lordship was singing at the top of lungs for some time before. All of us inside of the coach heard him as plain as a pikestaff. Very pretty it was, too," said the gentleman who had been pointed out as Mr. Nickleby. He belatedly made a bow in Judith's direction.

Judith's gaze traveled on to study the face of his young lordship, who had flushed when he came under discussion but whose dignity was such that he would not offer a word in his own defense. "Lord Baltor. Your servant, ma'am," he said, making a creditable bow despite the obvious headache that he sported.

The slight gentleman who stood next to Lord Baltor, and who up to that point had not addressed anyone but the butler, also bowed to Judith and mumbled something incoherent that she took as a pleasantry of some sort.

"Miss Grantham, these persons say that according to the innkeeper's wife, you graciously opened Elmswood Hall to unfortunate travelers," said Withers in a wooden voice.

Judith was puzzled for only a moment before she recalled her jesting remark to Cecily about wishing for a handful of marooned guests. Looking at the motley foursome in the hall, Judith thought wryly that her offhand wish had just been granted. Certainly, she could not turn them away since the inn was full. But surely there had been one or two other passengers on the ditched mail coach, she thought, when she did not see the gentleman of the bleeding brow. "Is this all of you?" she asked.

Her question seemed to relieve the tension of those who looked at her. "Aye, Miss Grantham. The others were able to double up in the rooms or bed down in the coffee room in front of the fire," said Mr. Nickleby.

"But that was not for me, as I told Mr. Nickleby," said Mrs. Nickleby. "I said that since a lady had been so gracious as to open her home, it would fairly rude not to give her ladyship the satisfaction of helping those less fortunate than herself."

"I appreciate your kind thought, Mrs. Nickleby," said Judith, a decided gleam in her fine eyes. Before her unlooked-for guests could realize that she viewed their advent on her doorstep with amusement, she gestured toward the drawing room. "A cold collation and tea is served in the drawing room. I assume that you must all be famished after such an arduous day and I invite you to make free. I shall have rooms prepared for you in the meantime."

"There now, Henry. Did I not tell you that we would not make fools of ourselves?" asked Mrs. Nickleby complacently, leading the way into the drawing room. Her husband's reply was lost as he followed his spouse. The slight gentleman, rubbing his hands together in obvious anticipation, lost little time in ducking after the Nicklebys. Lord Baltor alone hesitated, his lip unconsciously caught between his teeth as he looked uncertainly at his hostess.

Judith smiled serenely at his lordship. "I shall not keep you from supper, Lord Baltor." He flushed again and went with a hasty step into the drawing room.

The butler could scarcely contain himself. "You are never sitting down with that lot, Miss Grantham!"

"Oh, I don't know. It might be rather diverting. I have never dined with tradespeople before," said Judith. She had divined at one glance that the Nicklebys were of the rising middle class.

"Cits, and likely thieves to boot," said Withers sweepingly.

Judith laughed. "You have forgotten poor Lord Baltor. Really, Withers, it would be frightfully rude to abandon my unexpected guests because they chance not to run in the same circles as I do. Has Miss Brown come down yet?"

The butler shook his head. "The maid who was sent in to Miss Brown found her asleep on top of the bed, still in her travel dress. She thought she should not wake the young miss."

"Quite right. I could see that the poor girl was dead on her feet. I shall look in on her later to see that she is comfortable," said Judith, nodding. With every expectation of being entertained, she went into the drawing room;

It always pleased Judith to see her home done up for the holiday season and in particular the drawing room. Garlands of bay, fir, rosemary, and pine twigs offset by red silk bows looped across the mantel and several branches of candles burned with cheery light. From the ceiling hung the traditional kissing bough of fragrant greenery adorned with candles, red apples, rosettes of colored paper, and various ornaments. A bunch of gray-green mistletoe laden with white berries was at its center. All in all, the scene was a decidedly cozy one, what with the addition of her unexpected houseguests to complete the atmosphere of seasonal cheer, Judith thought.

Her guests had taken her at her word and had helped themselves to the cold meats and cheeses and bread that had been meant for her own supper. Mr. and Mrs. Nickleby had established themselves well in front of the fireplace where they could be certain of feeling the heat. The slight gentleman, who had not yet introduced himself, Judith remembered, had taken up a place a little separate from the others, apparently preferring to stand in the shadows of the curtained windows and holding his heaping plate in his hands. Lord Baltor sat on the settee, obviously ill at ease and with only a meager cup of tea.

Mrs. Nickleby was recommending in almost a maternal fashion that he should eat at least a crust of bread. "For I know for a fact that one does not sleep half as well on an empty belly, your lordship," she said authoritatively, carrying a generous portion of lavishly buttered bread to her mouth.

"Quite right, pet," said Mr. Nickleby, nodding.

Upon catching sight of Judith, Lord Baltor leaped up from his seat with an expression almost of relief. "Miss Grantham!" he uttered.

Judith went forward, an easy smile on her face. "I trust all is to satisfaction," she said with an encompassing glance about her guests.

"Indeed it is, miss," said Mr. Nickleby. He was making inroads on a heavily loaded plate and he barely glanced up. Mrs. Nickleby, her mouth full, satisfied herself with a vigorous nod and a wave of what remained of her thick slab of bread. The slight gentleman nodded deferentially, but he did not vouchsafe a syllable.

Judith turned her smile on Lord Baltor. Without seeming to stare, she took notice of his reddened eyes and haggard face. "Pray join me in getting a plate, my lord. I am persuaded you must be at least as famished as I am."

Lord Baltor turned a shade green at the thought of putting food into his queasy stomach. "No, I think not at the moment. I-I prefer the tea, thank you."

"Then you must have a refill. Allow me to pour it for you," said Judith, turning to the sideboard and the tea pot. Lord Baltor followed her, voicing disjointed phrases of thanks. Judith responded soothingly as she poured tea for his lordship and of herself. She sipped at her cup and then asked in a lowered voice, "My lord, you appear a trifle pale. May I offer you a headache powder before you retire tonight?"

Lord Baltor flushed. "You are most kind, Miss Grantham." He summoned up a wavering smile and met her curious gaze frankly. "It was only a bit of a lark, you know. I never intended – that is to say, the coach swung too wide in the turn and before I knew it, we were all flung into the drift."

Judith did not comment on the young gentleman's obvious state of inebriation at the time, but instead asked, "Where are you bound, my lord?"

He seemed relieved that she did not pursue the cause of the accident. "I was supposed to visit with friends the entire break between terms, but I am going home for the remainder of the holiday. It is to be a surprise to my aunt, who is all the family I have in the world. She is a wonderful old lady."

"I am certain that she shall be most happy to see you," said Judith. She was on the point of saying something further, but her attention was claimed by Mrs. Nickleby, who proposed that a card gave be got up as the evening was still young. Judith thought there was a point at which even she drew the line. "Thank you, but you must not count on me, ma'am. It has been a rather fatiguing day, as I am persuaded you must understand, having traveled also. I shall say good night to you all now, and my butler will show you up to your rooms whenever you are ready."

"Well, that is as strong a hint as I ever heard," said Mrs. Nickleby, somewhat affronted.

"I am persuaded Miss Grantham meant nothing by it, so kind as she has been, dear wife," said Mr. Nickleby, setting aside an emptied plate with a replete sigh. He cracked a huge yawn. "Truth to tell, pet, I am that ready for a soft bed myself."

Mrs. Nickleby's expression softened. "Of course, Mr. Nickleby. Anyone can see that you are dead on your feet." The couple made their good nights to the company and went out of the drawing room, Mrs. Nickleby exclaiming all the while that she hoped the bed was not too soft or her back would suffer. "And one cannot tell what one may find in a strange place. I shall myself inspect the freshness of the sheets. You know what is said of these great houses, Mr. Nickleby. The rooms are done up and then left for months on end without airing."

Judith and Lord Baltor exchanged speaking glances. A soft cough claimed their attention and they both glanced with surprise at the slight gentleman, who had been so unassuming as to have been forgotten. "Begging your pardon, miss, but I was wishful of thanking you for a fine supper," he said.

"You are most welcome, Mr. – I am sorry, but I do not know your name," said Judith.

There was almost an imperceptible hesitation before the slight gentleman bowed. "I am John Smith, at your service, miss."

Judith's gray eyes lit with amusement. It was obvious that the slight gentleman had chosen to offer to her a pseudonym and she wondered for what reason. He appeared a most harmless sort. "Of course, Mr. Smith. We shall undoubtedly visit again on the morrow, if this weather has anything to say of the matter. Normally one cannot hear the wind so plainly in this room."

"Indeed, miss," said Mr. Smith. He bowed again and left the drawing room.

Lord Baltor offered his arm. "I would count it an honor to be allowed to escort you, Miss Grantham," he said formally.

Judith inclined her head, again amused. Despite his lordship's wearying day and the persistent headache, he was no less mannered than his birth would allow him to be. She accepted his escort and they left the drawing room together, to separate at the head of the stairs where Judith left him to the guidance of a footman and went on to her own bedroom. It had been an interesting end to what had begun as a rather depressing day.

Judith, who was reminded by the rumble in her stomach that she had not eaten anything while downstairs, requested that a cup of broth and sandwich be brought to her room. Not even the enticement of a supper would have persuaded her to remain in the drawing room and in peril of being roped into a card game with Mrs. Nickleby, who was surely one of the most vulgar individuals she had ever met.

Chapter Four

Judith was never at her best in the morning, yet she detested remaining late abed. It was therefore her custom to take breakfast alone in the breakfast room, in blessed quiet with a large pot of coffee at her elbow and the view through the French windows of Elmswood's snow-covered lawn to soothe her jaundiced eyes. The servants had long since become aware of her distaste for speech in the morning and they always served her with silent efficiency before leaving her to her sluggish thoughts. Judith appreciated and even looked forward to this golden hour when she could literally waken slowly to the rest of the world.

With guests in the house, her usual routine would be next to impossible to maintain. Judith did not think that she could bring herself to face the voluble Mrs. Nickleby over the breakfast table. But she could not remain in her bedroom either, for to do so would make her feel unnecessarily claustrophobic. She hoped that by going down to breakfast at a particularly early hour she would be less likely to run into any of her assorted guests and would still be able to enjoy her usual solitary beginning to the day.

She did not bargain on someone being before her in the breakfast room, and especially not the gentleman she found. At sight of him, she stopped dead in her tracks. The hawkish features and the broad-shouldered, lithe body were all too familiar to her. An almost incoherent sound escaped her.

Sir Peregrine Ashford was in a foul temper. The day before he had spent hours out in the freezing weather chasing down a foolish chit of a girl. He had thought when he reached the posting house that his pursuit had finally come to an end, but the intelligence that the young lady had been taken up by Miss Grantham had sent him once more out into the heavy swirling snow.

When he had at last caught up with his prey, he had been obliged to bang on the door of a private residence at the ungodly hour of midnight and demand admittance, which had been granted to him with astonished dismay. He had risen early after an indifferent sleep, determined to quit Elmswood Hall as swiftly as possible and get on with his business. But he had been informed somewhat unhappily by the butler that the house was snowbound. Sir Peregrine had not accepted the news with equanimity.

He felt that the situation could not be worse, until he looked up from his breakfast and met the startled gaze of the woman who had once jilted him. His smile was sardonic. He had been prepared for this encounter, though perhaps it had come earlier than he had anticipated. "Good morning, Miss Grantham. I trust that you slept well," he said with the manner of a perfect guest. But he did not rise to offer his hostess a chair, instead leaning back a little in his own so that he could survey her better.

Judith had gone rather white, but she managed to nod coolly at him. She approached the table and seated herself. It took all her fortitude not to allow how shaken she was by this totally unexpected encounter to show. "Sir Peregrine, this is quite a surprise. I had no notion of your arrival," she said, and knew instantly how inane and inadequate were the words. Questions tumbled through her still sleep-fogged mind. She knew that she must get hold of herself, and quickly. Desperately, she looked about and she seized gratefully upon the coffee pot.

"Meaning that if you had known you would have given orders to bar the door against me, leaving me to freeze slowly on the steps," said Sir Peregrine.

Judith could not stop the faintest tremor of her hand as she poured steaming coffee into her cup. Anger at herself for the slight betrayal steadied her nerves. She cast an irritated glance at her companion. "How idiotic! Of course, I would not have. Though if you mean to rip up at me this early in the morning, I shall probably wish that I had had the opportunity."

Sir Peregrine smiled, though with little amusement. "You have always been quick to take fire, Judith."

"And you, sir, have always had the singular knack of setting up my back," said Judith swiftly. All her hopes of a quiet easing into the day had vanished with Sir Peregrine's unexpected presence, and that did nothing to improve her overall mood. She eyed him in a decidedly unfriendly way. "Why have you come to Elmswood? I do not mind telling you, it is an unpleasant shock to discover you at the breakfast table." She was still thinking of her lost solitude and therefore his reaction caught her by surprise.

"Thank you, ma'am! I had long ago been brought to realize that you held me in contempt, but I was not aware of those feelings of revulsion that you have harbored," said Sir Peregrine. His piercing blue eyes were bright and hard.

Judith flushed, realizing belatedly how uncivil she had sounded. She had always prided herself on treating others as kindly as she herself would like to be treated. No matter what history lay between herself and Sir Peregrine, it did not give her license to insult him unnecessarily. "I am sorry. I was unforgivably rude. My excuse must be that I am not at my best in the morning. I am not usually so prickly after I have had my coffee."

Sir Peregrine stared at her. After a long moment he allowed a fleeting grin to cross his face. "I have overset your hopes of a solitary breakfast, have I? If it will ease your disgruntlement in any measure, I was not best pleased to have my own breakfast interrupted. I detest making conversation so early in the day."

"And so do I," said Judith.

He laughed and turned his attention to his unfinished plate, obviously with the intention of suspending communication until they were both ready to resume it.

Judith helped herself to eggs and ham and then set to with relish, finding that she had quite an appetite after her light repast the night before. She finished eating and began her second cup of coffee in the ensuing silence. Over the cup's rim she watched Sir Peregrine begin on a second helping of steak and kidneys.

Finally, she sighed. "It is of no use, Perry. I still wish to know why you have come to Elmswood. You cannot have a sudden uncontrollable desire for my company."

She meant the last to be a light touch of humor, but when she looked into his suddenly frowning eyes, it occurred to her that it would not be such a bad thing if he had come with the object of seeking her out.

Sir Peregrine was apparently not subject to the same wistful thought. "Believe me, nothing short of necessity would have brought me to Elmswood Hall. I was informed at the posting house that you arrived there with a young lady who was subsequently persuaded to come on with you here. I believe that you are harboring my ward, Miss Grantham."

Judith, who had flinched at Sir Peregrine's blunt disclaimer, now looked at him in stupefaction. "You? You are the beastly, overbearing cousin that that poor girl is fleeing? I cannot credit it."

"Indeed, can you not?" Sir Peregrine's smile was grim. "I am certain that Cecily has spun a fine tale for you, but do now allow her to play too strongly on your sympathies. She is too young to know what she is about, besides possessing a decided turn for the dramatic. I have had little ease of mind since succeeding to her guardianship. If the truth be known, I would like to wash my hands of the business."

Judith had listened to him with increasing stiffness. Everything he said seemed to confirm Cecily's assertions. "I am persuaded that you do not mean that. Surely you are not grown so callous that you have forgotten what dreams one may hold at age seventeen! Of course, the girl is high-spirited and romantic. What young girl is not?"

"I was never a dreamy youth, even in my salad days. And you, dear Judith, did not allow romantic fancy to turn *your* head. Indeed, far from it. I doubt there was ever a more prosaic young lady in all of England," said Sir Peregrine with irony.

Judith bit back the impulsive retort she was about to utter. It would not do to cup up at Sir Peregrine over the past, not if she was to discover how best to aid Cecily out of her predicament. She took a deep breath to calm herself, though Sir Peregrine's unfair observation stung. "Cecily is still a child, I grant you, but there is a hint of fortitude, of determination, about her that is appealing. My interest was caught by her story of an unwanted suitor and an overbearing guardian. However, I certainly do not approve of the course of action she has taken, and I hope that while you are here, Sir Peregrine, you and Cecily may iron out some of your differences."

"Your concern is misplaced and misguided, ma'am. I think that I know better how to deal with Cecily than would a stranger," said Sir Peregrine coolly.

Judith lost her temper. "Indeed, and see what has come of your handling of her! She was fleeing from you in a common mail coach, intending to solicit a position as a lady's maid. I do not pretend to understand the desperation of a gently bred girl who feels compelled to such a course, but I do think that if you had had an ounce of common sense you would have attempted to sound out her feelings before –"

"My God, do you think that I have not tried reason? But it is akin to addressing a whirligig. My precious ward has tumbled headlong into love not fewer than six times in two years. The last was the dancing master at her boarding school, who, I am given to understand, thought it might be lucrative to encourage the simpering adoration of an heiress," said Sir Peregrine. He gave a short bark of laughter. "Cecily was not best pleased to learn that her inamorata chose a purse of silver and flight over the less charming prospect of enduring penury with her."

The years rushed over Judith, an echo of long-ago hurt. "How odd that you should choose the same means to direct Cecily's destiny," she said with a brittle smile. Her gray eyes had lightened almost to transparency, so great was her fury.

Sir Peregrine was taken aback by the sudden blaze of passion in her expression. He was given no opportunity to question her oblique statement, however, as the breakfast room door opened and a man and woman unknown to him entered.

At sight of Judith, Mr. Nickleby smiled and nodded. "There you are, Mrs. Nickleby. Did I not tell you that early hours are kept in the country? We have almost missed breakfast with our kind hostess. Your servant, Miss Grantham, sir," said Mr. Nickleby, making a courtly bow to the two who were sitting silent at the table. If he had been a sensitive man he would have been struck by the electric tension in the room, but as it was, he never noticed the flush of temper in Miss Grantham's face or the coldness in the gentleman's expression.

He held a chair for Mrs. Nickleby, who seated herself with a sniff of disapproval. "I cannot for the life of me understand why some insist on breakfast at the crack of dawn, and then it must be kippers and eggs. So heavy and unhealthy for one, I am persuaded. I myself take only chocolate and toast. Mr. Nickleby, I do not see any chocolate. It must be an oversight, surely. Pray pull the bell and have a pot brought." She glanced across the table and her brows rose. "Miss Grantham, you are not leaving us surely?"

Judith, who had arisen from her seat, paused momentarily. Her eyes glittered. "Mrs. Nickleby, allow me to make known to you Sir Peregrine Ashford, who arrived some time in the night. I am persuaded that he will be spellbound by the story of your unlucky trip on the mail coach. Pray do excuse me, but I have a hundred and one items to see to this morning." She swept out of the breakfast room, deriving a certain satisfaction at leaving Sir Peregrine to the Nicklebys and their unceasing conversation this early in the day. She hoped that it would give him a fine case of indigestion.

Chapter Five

Judith went upstairs at once. She knocked at Cecily's door and, at her soft invitation, entered the bedroom. Cecily was sitting before the cheval glass while a maid put the finishing touches to the heavy curls that had been swept back and were held away from her face by a bright pink riband. The result was not unlike a soft dark cloud framing Cecily's huge eyes and heart-shaped face. Judith thought that she had never seen a more beautiful girl.

Cecily leaped up at once when she saw her hostess in the glass. She held out her hands. "Miss Grantham! I do apologize for falling asleep last night when I was to join you. It was just that I was so sleepy and I thought that I would close my eyes for only a moment. When I awakened, it was morning! I was never so mortified."

Judith pressed Cecily's fingers briefly before letting go her hands. Laughing, she said, "Never mind, dear girl. I shan't eat you."

"How well I know that! You have been all that is kind," said Cecily, looking at her with gratitude.

Judith sighed. She gestured for the maid to go and when they were alone, she said, "Cecily, I must tell you that Sir Peregrine is here."

The normal color was driven from the girl's cheeks, leaving a hectic patch high on each rounded cheek. "Here! But he cannot be. How ever did he find me so quickly? Oh, Miss Grantham! I beg of you, do not allow him to take me away. I shall be so desperately unhappy. You have no notion what he is like when he is angered."

"Oh, don't I just?" uttered Judith under her breath. The whole encounter with Sir Peregrine had left her seething, and she was not at

all repentant that she had saddled him with the Nicklebys. She saw that
Cecily was looking questioningly at her and she pushed aside her own
perturbation to answer. "My dear girl, I have no right to keep you from
your guardian, if such he is."

Cecily took a step backward and regarded Judith with a look of
betrayal. "I had thought of you as my friend."

"And I trust that I am still." Judith saw that Cecily was regarding
her with the old wariness and she said urgently, "Cecily, you must see
that I have no choice in this. Why, Sir Peregrine would have every right
to call in a constable if I were to deny you to him. You shall simply have
to meet with him."

"No, no! I cannot. He has such a *cutting* way about him, you see.
He makes me feel so awkward and inadequate that I become tangled in
knots whenever I try to speak to him," said Cecily.

Judith felt sympathy for the young girl's plight. She also had once
been too reticent and shy to express herself well. And that inability had
cost her dear. "If you wish it, I shall go with you when you meet with Sir
Peregrine. I shan't allow anyone underneath my roof to be browbeaten,
I promise you."

Cecily shook her head quickly. "Miss Grantham, I beg of you, if
you will not shelter me from my cousin, at least lend me a chaise. I shall
be gone in a trice and I will send your carriage back the instant that I
have found a mail coach to London. Just give me an hour or two before
telling Sir Peregrine that I am gone."

"It is out of the question. Even if I were inclined to do anything so
absurd, it would not serve you. We are all snowbound and likely to be
for the remainder of the day," said Judith.

She watched as Cecily flew to the window and lifted the curtain.
She was not entirely amused by the girl's bitten-off exclamation and the
stomping of one dainty foot. "Cecily, you really have no choice but to
speak to Sir Peregrine. Perhaps this is just the opportunity you have

needed to set things right between the two of you, since you both are forced to remain at Elmswood for the time being."

Cecily turned swiftly. She was flushed. "Nothing could persuade me to step foot into the same room with Sir Peregrine. I shall remain upstairs."

Judith experienced a feeling of disappointment. "I am sorry for that, Cecily. I had thought you possessed more courage. But I see now that I was mistaken." She turned and left the bedroom, leaving Cecily to stare after her in astonishment and gathering gudgeon.

Judith slowly made her way downstairs, her brows knit. She did not know what to do about the standoff between Cecily and Sir Peregrine. But fortunately, it was not her problem and she could easily wash her hands of it, she told herself, though without much success. How ever much Cecily behaved in just the sort of dramatic, childish fashion that Sir Peregrine had said to expect of her, Judith could not but wonder if there was not more substance to the girl. Her own initial impression could not be entirely incorrect.

Judith reached the bottom of the stairs before she recalled her other guests. She hesitated, not wanting to walk in on the Nicklebys or for that matter Sir Peregrine Ashford. She had had quite enough of high drama and absurdity for one morning. Indeed, she had the unmistakable beginnings of the headache. What she required was quiet and a chance to order her thoughts, she told herself.

Withers had seen Judith descend the stars and his sympathy was aroused by her worried frown. He had heard through the servants' grapevine that Miss Grantham had been up to see Miss Brown. Obviously, her visit to that young lady had not gone well. He stepped forward. "Is there anything you wish, miss?"

Judith smiled, a rueful light in her eyes. "There is, actually. Where may I be private from my various assorted guests, Withers?"

The butler's expression reflected his complete understanding. "The library, miss. I have not seen anyone enter that particular room, though some persons have taken it upon themselves to inspect the premises," he said in censorious tones.

Judith laughed, before recalling that she did not want to be found. She glanced about hastily. "Why is it that I feel a fugitive in my own home? Withers, I should like a lemon water and a headache powder in the library, please."

"Very good, miss," said Withers.

Judith entered the library and closed the door behind her with a sigh. She turned to seek one of the wing chairs before the grate, behind which crackled a welcoming fire. She was just seating herself when out of the corner of her eye she caught a flicker of movement. Judith turned her head, but finding nothing out of the ordinary in the curtained window or the shelves of books, she put back her head and closed her eyes. It was as she began dozing off that she heard a whisper of sound. Judith started up, her eyes flying wide.

Mr. Smith stood awkwardly in the midst of the carpet, a vaguely furtive look on his face. "Begging your pardon, miss. It weren't my intention to startle you."

Judith's heart was racing. She swallowed. "Where did you come from, Mr. Smith?" she asked sharply.

Mr. Smith's expression became sheepish. "I was perusing the titles, as it were, when you came in, miss. I saw immediately that you had not seen me and I was about to bring myself to your attention when you sat down all tired-like and closed your eyes. Not wishing to disturb you, miss, I thought I would tiptoe away and leave you to it."

It was more than Judith had ever heard the gentleman utter at any one time and definitely more than she wanted to hear at that moment. She put her hand to her head. "Mr. Smith, I appreciate your consideration. However, do keep in mind that on any given day I for one would prefer to be civilly disturbed rather than half frightened out of my wits."

The library door opened and Withers entered, a silver tray in his hands. He paused when he saw that his mistress was not alone as he had expected. Mr. Smith seized his moment. "I shall remember it, miss. I perceive that you have called for refreshment and so I will be running along now." He sidled past the butler and whisked himself out of the door, without seeming in any great hurry but yet moving with speed.

Withers looked around at his mistress. "That is a very odd gentleman, if you'll pardon my saying so, Miss Grantham."

"Indeed, he is," said Judith, reflecting that Mr. Smith was not the only guest whose behavior was extraordinary. She shook her head on a sigh. "I do not know what I have done to deserve all of this."

Withers made a commiserating noise. He set the tray with its glass of lemon water and the packet of powder on an occasional table and straightened up. "Is there anything else that you require, miss?"

"No, Withers, that will be all, thank you," said Judith.

The butler left her alone, closing the door softly behind him, and relayed quietly to the footmen that Miss Grantham was not to be disturbed. Any persons found near the library were to be firmly steered away and if anyone was to inquire after Miss Grantham, they were to be given the reply that she was consulting with the housekeeper. That should do it, thought Withers with satisfaction.

But he did not take into account that Miss Grantham's nature was fairly well known to one particular gentleman, who snorted with derision when he was given the housekeeper excuse and with very little reflection hit upon the library as the most likely place that Miss Grantham would secrete herself. Sir Peregrine marched toward the closed door, brushing aside all efforts by a conscientious footman to turn him away, and thrust open the door.

Judith looked up from the book in her hands, startled. During an hour and a half of blessed solitude, her nerves had steadied and her headache had dissipated almost to nonexistence. It was therefore an unpleasant shock to see Sir Peregrine standing so aggressively in the doorway, his expression both grim and triumphant. The question of Cecily's well-being, which had receded proportionately with the interest she had found in her book, came rushing back to the fore. "Bother," said Judith under her breath. She summoned a polite smile to her lips. "Sir Peregrine. How...nice."

He laughed at her intonation and came forward. "Quite so. But you should have known that I was not to be hoodwinked so easily, Miss Grantham. Your estimable housekeeper hardly needs such strict guidance as your footman tried to persuade me into believing."

The footman in question hovered anxiously about the open door. Judith, who realized at once that her household had been attempting to shield her, gave a reassuring nod to him. "You may go, Henry. I shall speak to Sir Peregrine." The footman reached for the brass knob and closed the door.

Sir Peregrine walked to the mantel and leaned his shoulder against it, not bothering to move aside the fir and holly that decorated it. The scent from the bruised greenery became pungent on the air. "Kind of you to grant me an audience, ma'am," he said with irony.

Judith marked her place in the book and closed it. "What may I do for you, Sir Peregrine?"

Sir Peregrine came away from the mantel and seated himself in the wing chair opposite her, crossing one knee over the other. His booted toe swung gently. "I first wish to convey an apology, Miss Grantham. I realized after your precipitate exit from the breakfast room this morning that I was perhaps harsher in my speech with you than I had any right to be. I hope that we may begin again, and with greater civility."

Judith was silent a moment. Her eyes were unreadable. "Of course, Sir Peregrine. I certainly will not cast aside such a handsome apology."

"You revenged yourself upon me finely, you know," said Sir Peregrine reflectively. "I never in my life wish to hear a single word more regarding mail coaches and their attendant discomforts and dangers."

That brought a laugh from Judith. Her eyes sparkled, having lost their shuttered look. "I suppose I should apologize for that. It was very bad of me, I fear."

Sir Peregrine agreed with the faintest of grins. "But you were always one for pranks, were you not? It was one of your most likeable qualities."

The easy smile was wiped from Judith's face and her expression became notably cooler. "What is it you wished to speak to me about, Sir Peregrine?"

Sir Peregrine mentally cursed himself for the misstep. He had wanted to disarm her and sweep away the barrier that she had erected between them so that his task of persuading her to his viewpoint would be easier. Now the barrier was firmly entrenched and he thought that there would be little use in gentle, logical persuasion. He decided on a frontal assault. "Miss Grantham, once more you have anticipated me. I think that you may guess what I wish to address, and that is your obvious hampering of my efforts to establish an understanding with my ward, Miss Cecily Brown."

"I? You mistake, sir. I have done nothing to *hamper* you, as you put it. Quite the contrary, in fact."

"Come, Miss Grantham! I have sent word up to Cecily twice that I awaited her and both times she sent back a refusal to see me. I know well where your sympathies lie and also your disapproval of my intentions for my ward's future. Surely you do not intend to deny that you have brought influence upon Cecily," said Sir Peregrine with impatience.

Judith stared at him with distant coldness. "My dear sir, your opinion of my character is most gratifying, to be sure. You accuse me of harboring your ward, recommending to her that she have nothing whatsoever to do with you, and generally flying in the face of all that is honorable and lawful!"

She rose quickly to her feet, the book sliding unheeded from her lap to the carpet. Her heated emotion had brought becoming color into her cheeks. "I do not blame Cecily in the least for refusing to deal with you, for you are too cloth-headed to entertain the least understanding of anyone but you!" She spun on her heel, intending to leave his presence.

But Sir Peregrine, having leaped to his feet, caught hold of her arm and turned her ungently about. Her angry gaze met his hard, blue eyes. "Judith!"

"Unhand me this instant!" exclaimed Judith. She tried to pull free of his grasp, but his fingers only tightened on her arm. The situation was intolerable. Furious, she slapped his face with every ounce of her strength.

"Damn you, Judith!" he exclaimed. His hands slid up to her shoulders and he gave her a quick, hard shake. They stared at one another then, tension crackling between them.

Sir Peregrine found that he could not look away from her eyes or her whitened face. The years had rolled back for him and he no longer remembered his ward. All he was aware of was the breath coming quickly between Judith's half-parted lips, the feel of her slender bones under his hands.

The spell was broken by a knock on the library door.

Sir Peregrine slowly loosened his fingers from her shoulders. Judith stepped back, her eyes still on his face. Sir Peregrine turned away to the mantel, as though he had been contemplating the fire for several minutes.

Judith took a shuddering breath. She was unutterably shaken. A second knock sounded and she found her voice. "Enter!"

The door opened and Withers stepped inside, his expression giving nothing away, but when he spoke there was a thread of anxiety in his voice. His eyes went from his mistress to Sir Peregrine's broad shoulders and back again. "Miss Grantham, I am sorry to intrude, but there is a problem that Cook would like to consult with you about."

"Yes, I shall come immediately," said Judith. She was immeasurably relieved that she was not to be faced with dealing with the tumult of emotions she was feeling at just that moment. She went quickly out of the library.

Sir Peregrine did not look around at her exit.

Chapter Six

Judith dealt with the minor culinary emergency, smoothing Cook's affront at having her kitchen invaded by Mrs. Nickleby and being told in lofty tones that her pudding was off. "I ask you, miss! My pudding has never been off and so I told that nosey-body to her face, *which* she did not care for, you may be sure of that!"

"No, Cook, I am certain that she did not," said Judith with a sigh, sensing that she would have further calming to do whenever she should meet Mrs. Nickleby. And that would undoubtedly be at luncheon, she realized. She wondered dismally what had happened to the dull quiet that she was used to whenever she returned to Elmswood from one of her visits.

When Judith left the kitchen, she went directly upstairs and ordered a bath. She told her maid that under no circumstances did she want to be disturbed until it was time to dress for luncheon. The maid was astonished that her mistress would shut herself up when there were guests in the house and she was not behind in mentioning it in the servants' hall when she went down to request hot water to be brought up.

After several sympathetic observations and sighs, it was the consensus of the household that Miss Grantham's holiday was not quite what it should be, what with vulgar tradespeople running tame in the house, a suspicious shadow of a man snooping about, and a runaway heiress kicking up a dust. Not to mention the disturbing presence of the gentleman who had once broken Miss Grantham's heart.

Perhaps fortunately, Judith was unaware that she was the prime topic of conversation below-stairs. She took her time in her bath. She had much to think about, primarily of how a certain gentleman made her feel whenever he looked at her.

Since she had jilted Sir Peregrine five years before, they had met one another on numerous occasions at London functions to which they had both been invited. She had always been able to prepare herself for those moments, only to be expected since she and Sir Peregrine were members of the same social circle. Those fleeting meetings had always been made easier by the tacit understand of their peers that Miss Grantham and Sir Peregrine Ashford were never to be seated together at dinner or left without other partners during a ballroom dance.

She had come to rely on that distance to preserve herself from pain, Judith realized. When she had come so unexpectedly upon Sir Peregrine at her own breakfast table, she had come close to fainting away from the shock. Their relationship had undeniably not improved through that distancing. They had immediately cut up at one another in such a horrid manner that Judith could only wonder what had become of their social breeding.

But the worst moments had been those in the library. When Sir Peregrine had taken hold of her, time was flung aside as though it did not exist, and she had felt everything for him that she had felt for him before. He infuriated her, teased her, made her love him. And that was the crux of the matter, thought Judith bleakly. She had been fooling herself for a very long time. She did still love him. In those moments when her gaze was locked with his, she had seen something stir in his piercing eyes. She had sensed the precipice yawning before them, and had welcomed it. Then Withers' knock had come and the moment had been lost.

Judith sighed. She was not certain whether she ought to be glad for it or regret that Sir Peregrine had not kissed her. However, at this point it was all rather academic. The snow would let up and Sir Peregrine would bundle Cecily into his carriage and be off with never a backward look.

It was a thoroughly depressing thought.

Judith decided that she had wallowed long enough, both in her unproductive thoughts and in her bath. She toweled dry and pulled the bell rope to summon her maid. It was time to dress for luncheon. Actually, it might be a welcome diversion to sit down with her disparate guests.

An hour later, Judith wondered how she could have harbored such a hopeful thought. Before she had even entered the dining room, Mrs. Nickleby had latched onto her sleeve and proceeded to bend her ear regarding her cook's attitude.

"Insufferable, Miss Grantham, I assure you! The woman positively *threatened* to throw me out of the kitchen on my ear. Why, I was never more surprised in my life, when all I had done was to offer a bit of well-meant advice," said Mrs. Nickleby.

"That you have a talent for, pet," said Mr. Nickleby.

Judith glanced at the man, wondering if he was deliberately stoking the fire of his wife's wrath, but Mr. Nickleby's expression was as pleasant and complacent as usual. She returned her attention to Mrs. Nickleby and once more attempted to bring reason into play. "Mrs. Nickleby, surely you must understand that the kitchen is Cook's domain. I am certain that there is an area in your life you must care greatly for and that it would give you pain to have someone, perhaps less knowledgeable than- "

"Less knowledgeable! Begging your pardon, Miss Grantham, but I am a superb cook," uttered Mrs. Nickleby. She looked to her husband for confirmation and he willingly gave it, patting his ample waistline in testimony. "That you are, pet," he said.

Judith glanced about helplessly. At this rate, none of them would ever get to the table, she thought. And she could not simply withdraw from Mrs. Nickleby. The outrageous woman actually had hold of a bit of her sleeve, thought Judith in annoyance.

Judith's glance met that of Lord Baltor, and he comprehended the situation. He promptly stepped forward and his action edged Mrs. Nickleby back a half-step so that she was forced to drop her hand from Judith's sleeve. "Miss Grantham, allow me the privilege of escorting you into luncheon," he said, offering his arm to Judith.

She placed her fingers on his elbow and thanked him with a dazzling smile. Over her shoulder, she said composedly, "Do join Lord Baltor and me, Mrs. Nickleby. We are to have a delightful current pudding for dessert."

"Well!" exclaimed Mrs. Nickleby. "And here I have just been saying that the pudding is not fit to be spooned up."

Her spouse patted her reassuringly on the shoulder. "Never mind, pet. The Quality abide by their own rules," he said.

Mrs. Nickleby took his arm and lowered her voice to an octave that she mistakenly thought private. "I shall never be more glad of anything than to shake the dust of this house from my feet, Mr. Nickleby. I have never been subjected to ruder treatment. And as for the help! Why, what do you think? I discovered one of the maids going through the pockets of my best cloak. She excused herself by saying that she was looking for an extra button to sew on in place of one that has fallen off. I hope that I know better than to believe that tale! No one looks for work, now do they, Mr. Nickleby?"

"It is unfortunately true, pet," said Mr. Nickleby with a sigh. "Haven't I pointed out for years that very same thing in the clothier business?"

The Nicklebys' conversation carried them all into the dining room. Judith pretended not to hear. She was determined that the luncheon was to be a pleasant interlude. She quietly thanked Lord Baltor when he seated her and she was not unpleased that he took the chair beside her. She noticed when the slight gentleman slipped into place on her other side and she nodded pleasantly to him, not in any anxiety that she would offend if she did not verbally greet him. She had become used to Mr. Smith's quietude and she knew that her task of conversing with her table partners would be greatly reduced since Mr. Smith never put himself forward into any conversation.

While the Nicklebys seated themselves opposite, she leaned over toward Lord Baltor and said in a low voice, "I am unutterably relieved to have you for my partner at table, my lord. You have no notion how I shook at the thought of Mr. Nickleby, and just beyond him his good wife."

For the first time since Judith had met Lord Baltor, she saw an uninhibited smile on his face. "I consider it an equal protection, ma'am."

Judith laughed, almost surprised by the dry witticism. She had gathered that, sober, Lord Baltor was much too serious for his years. It pleased her that his lordship was capable of charm without first imbibing from a bottle. "I hope that I am to hear a rendition of a carol from you during your stay here at Elmswood. I, too, enjoy singing," said Judith, smiling.

Even as Lord Baltor flushed at her gentle teasing, his grin widened. All at once he looked his young years. "If you will but join me, Miss Grantham, I will endeavor to lift the ceiling."

"I shall hold you to that, my lord," said Judith. She had wondered at Sir Peregrine's absence and now she sensed rather than saw him enter the dining room. She turned her head.

He had paused in the doorway, sweeping the table with a glance and taking note that the only available place was beside Mrs. Nickleby. When his eyes met Judith's, her own sparked to amusement at his thinly veiled dismay. "Do pray join us, Sir Peregrine," she said, at her politest.

"Aye, do so," said Mrs. Nickleby, diverted from a running commentary on the centerpiece and those dishes that she could see on the sideboard by craning her neck. She smiled amiably and gestured at the place beside her. "There is ample elbow room, as you can see, Sir Peregrine."

"Thank you, Mrs. Nickleby. You are most kind," said Sir Peregrine hollowly.

With Sir Peregrine's sacrifice on the altar of good manners, Judith's spirits took an upturn for the better. The butler bent down to whisper in her ear that Miss Brown would not be joining the company for luncheon, preferring a tray in her bedroom. "Why does that not surprise me?" murmured Judith, not allowing herself to be in the least upset. She did, however, make a mental note to visit Cecily later in the afternoon.

The girl simply had to be brought to an understanding of her responsibilities, for nothing in the world would persuade Judith to go through another private interview with Sir Peregrine. She glanced down the table as the soup was served. Predictably, Mrs. Nickleby was addressing herself to anyone who was unfortunate to be within range. Judith smiled at Sir Peregrine's pained expression. She much preferred seeing that gentleman in public. It was so much kinder to her spirits, especially if he was to act as a buffer against Mrs. Nickleby's volubleness.

After luncheon, the company dispersed with various announced plans for passing the afternoon. Sir Peregrine and Lord Baltor discovered a mutual interest in billiards and went off to take a crack at the balls. Mr. Nickleby voiced a half-wish to join them, an aspiration quashed by his wife who scolded him for succumbing to what would surely become a gambling match. "For we all have heard what goes on in those clubs of the Quality," she said. He apologized for even thinking of indulging himself in such an evil and instead joined Mr. Smith in the library, each lying in an easy chair with a newspaper spread over his face that soon rose with rhythmic regularity. Mrs. Nickleby looked to Miss Grantham for what she termed a comfortable coze, but that lady firmly excused herself and took herself upstairs to visit with her recalcitrant guest.

In the hall Judith met the maid who was looking after Cecily. Noticing the still-laden luncheon tray in the woman's hands, Judith stopped her. "Hasn't Miss Brown any appetite?"

The maid shook her head. "The miss nibbled on naught but a cracker or two, Miss Grantham. And she took nothing but tea and dry toast for breakfast."

Judith quietly thanked the maidservant and walked on. Her brows had become knit by a small frown. Cecily had not had anything substantial to eat since before she had met her. Judith thought that was something else that must be addressed. She simply could not have the girl becoming ill, not with Sir Peregrine convinced that she was capable of contriving any sort of ruse to keep his ward from him.

Cecily granted Judith's entrance to the bedroom with a show of reluctance. "For I know why you have come, Miss Grantham. And I have not changed my mind by so much as a hair," she said. There was a spot of color high on her cheekbones as though she was flustered, but her eyes appeared bright with obstinacy.

It was not a promising beginning, but Judith was highly motivated to persuade the girl to at least a compromise. She seated herself in a wing chair in front of the grate, glancing up at the young girl as she did so. "Pray sit down, Cecily," she said quietly.

After a moment's hesitation, Cecily did as she was bid and perched on the edge of an accompanying chair. She folded her hands in her lap and her lashes dropped over the expression in her eyes.

Judith was not fooled into thinking that the girl was in any fashion cowed. She was beginning to see what Sir Peregrine had referred to when he had said the he had had difficulty in reaching Cecily.

Judith did not speak immediately, allowing her silence to work on the girl while she ordered her thoughts. Cecily was beginning to cast up quick curious glances when Judith at last addressed her. "Cecily,

I perfectly understand the reasons behind your reluctance in meeting with Sir Peregrine. He has undoubtedly treated you with a great deal of unfairness."

Cecily looked full at her, with surprise mirrored in her extraordinarily fringed, china-blue eyes. "I-I do not know what to say, Miss Grantham."

Judith held up her hand. "Pray allow me to finish. I have had occasion to converse with Sir Peregrine and certainly he is not the...easiest personage to deal with. However, I do believe that you must think of your best interests."

"My best interests?" faltered Cecily.

Judith nodded. "Quite so. Sir Peregrine is not likely to change his mind without good reason. I think that you have gained his attention by running away, but now you must capitalize on your position."

"Whatever are you talking about, Miss Grantham?" asked Cecily, bewildered. Her eyes suddenly widened. "Oh! Do you mean that I should threaten him?"

Judith shook her head, allowing a smile to flit over her face. "Not precisely that, no. But certainly, you must make it plain that the same determination that led you to run off will also lead you to cause him distress whenever a decision regarding your future is made without first consulting your opinion of the matter. And you must persuade Sir Peregrine of this without showing your fear of him."

"I am not precisely *frightened* of Perry," said Cecily haltingly.

"Then you do agree to meet with him while at Elmswood," said Judith. She watched as first astonishment, then comprehension flooded Cecily's expression.

"Oh! Of all the infamous tricks!" exclaimed Cecily.

"I am sorry to have had to trick you, Cecily, but I really felt that you gave me little choice in the matter," said Judith gently. "You see, if I allowed you to remain closeted away, then Sir Peregrine would almost certainly decide to come up himself and drag you from the bedroom.

I do not think in that instance that he would be open to anything that you might have to say."

Cecily stared at her thoughtfully. "You speak as though you know Sir Peregrine very well."

Judith stood up. "I shall expect you to come down and join us all for dinner this evening, Cecily. And in the meantime, I shall have a cup of broth sent up to you, for you are looking too pale." She turned to leave the bedroom, but she paused with her hand on the doorknob to glance back with the faintest lifting of her winged brows. "You know, I am so glad that my first impression of you was correct. I had thought you a determined and bright young woman. You have quite restored my faith in you."

Once more Cecily was left to stare after her, this time with much more food for thought, not the least of which was her hostess's declining to reply to her observation pertaining to Sir Peregrine.

Once downstairs, Judith busied herself in preparation for the traditional observance of Boxing Day. When her household had assembled, she handed out the gift boxes, taking a moment to address a personal word to each servant. It was a ceremony much enjoyed by all, including Judith. As always, she was glad that she had made the effort to return to Elmswood in time to uphold this particular tradition.

The boxing took longer than she had anticipated and she had to rush back upstairs to change in time for dinner. In the cheerful atmosphere generated by the boxing, she had forgotten the uncertain prospect before her in the dining room. There would likely be tension between Cecily and Sir Peregrine, as well as the usual reluctance of anyone to share table with Mrs. Nickleby, and she did not particularly look forward to the evening.

Chapter Seven

Judith had dreaded the half hour before dinner when all of her guests could be expected to assemble in the drawing room. But it went easier than she had expected, principally because the Nicklebys did not immediately appear. She was talking quietly with Lord Baltor and Sir Peregrine when Cecily came hesitantly through the door.

Judith knew that Cecily had entered when Lord Baltor's eyes flew wide and a stunned expression settled on his face. She rose and went toward the girl. "Cecily, my dear child," she said, holding out her hands.

Cecily grasped her fingers with almost a desperate grip and Judith looked searchingly at her. The girl appeared strained and her eyes were over-bright. Judith smiled reassuringly. "I shall stay right beside you," she murmured. Cecily cast up a grateful glance and allowed herself to be drawn toward the gentlemen.

Lord Baltor had leaped to his feet. His eyes had never left Cecily's face. His thoughts tumbled incoherently, but one remained crystal clear: He had never seen a more beautiful vision. When Judith brought Cecily up to him and introduced her, Lord Baltor accepted Cecily's hand almost with reverence. "Your servant, Miss Brown," he said in a strangled voice.

Cecily was not unused to admiration and she forgot her nervousness for a moment. She looked up at Lord Baltor with her wide innocent gaze. "I am so very glad to make your acquaintance, my lord," she said softly. She was quite taken with the manner in which Lord Baltor kissed her fingers and she was smiling as she reclaimed her hand.

But when she met the glance of her guardian, her smile faltered and a scared look entered her eyes. "Good-good evening, cousin," she stammered.

Sir Peregrine looked at her somewhat grimly. "You have led me a fine chase, Cecily. I hope that you are aware of the folly of your actions."

Cecily looked ready to sink into the carpet. Judith came to her support. "You shall be much better able to discuss these private matters at another time," she said firmly.

Sir Peregrine threw a piercing glance at Judith, who awaited his reaction with lifted brows. He seemed to reconsider whatever comment that he was on the point of making and instead nodded. "Miss Grantham for once is right. We shall speak after dinner, Cecily."

Lord Baltor had listened to the interchange with a gathering frown. He understood little but that somehow Sir Peregrine was related to this glorious creature and that she was frightened of his displeasure. When Lord Baltor looked into Cecily's piteous and lovely face, he was seized with a strong feeling of chivalry. He knew that he would do anything in his power to protect her from distress. "I hope that you will do me the honor of joining me at dinner," he said, addressing Cecily as though she was the only other individual in the room.

She nodded with a shy smile, soft color rising in her face. "You are most kind, my lord," she said, and placed her hand trustingly in his. The young couple drifted toward the settee, their heads inclined toward one another as they softly conversed.

Judith looked on with astonishment. Surely, she was not witnessing what she thought she was. It actually appeared to her that Cecily and Lord Baltor had fallen in love on the instant. When she glanced toward Sir Peregrine, she was annoyed to find that he had been waiting for her to do so, a faintly superior smile on his face. "You needn't look so smug, Perry," she said, unconsciously falling into her old habit of address.

Sir Peregrine noticed it, but he did not let on. "Needn't I? One so rarely is handed an opportunity to be able to point out one's infallibility. I did mention, did I not, that Cecily had been in love half a dozen times in two years? I was certain that I had. Do pray correct me if I am mistaken."

Judith surrendered the point with a laugh. "Oh, I would not date to counter your memory, sir."

"Would you not, Judith?" Sir Peregrine spoke quietly and there was a strangely intent look in his blue eyes.

Judith felt her heart turn over in her breast. "I-I think not," she said with an odd breathlessness.

Mr. Smith and the Nicklebys' came into the drawing room and Judith greeted their appearance almost with relief. She hid a shudder at Mrs. Nickleby's appearance. That lady had attired herself in a rich purple robe, a feathered velvet turban, and a ruby necklace that was matched by large rubies in her ears. An additional deep red stone flashed on the finger of one hand. The colors clashed hideously, thought Judith, but nothing of her opinion appeared on her pleasant countenance. "Here are the others. Pray excuse me, Sir Peregrine. There you are, Mr. and Mrs. Nickleby. And Mr. Smith, too! I see that Withers is ready for us. Shall we go to dinner?"

She was surprised when her elbow was taken in a firm grasp. In her ear was Sir Peregrine's civil voice. "I shall claim our fair hostess's company this evening, I believe." Judith looked up. She was quite unprepared for his cool smile or the challenge in his keen eyes.

"That is only proper, I am sure. You look a fine couple, too," said Mr. Nickleby approvingly. He did not appear to notice the slightest stiffening of Judith's frame. He held his arm out for his wife. "As splendid as you appear this evening in those shiny baubles, pet, I would not give you up if the Queen herself wished me to escort her."

Mrs. Nickleby tossed her head, pleased. The black feather in her turban waved above her deep-set eyes. "Why, Mr. Nickleby, I never!" For once she seemed to be content with the utterance of a mere phrase.

Judith and Sir Peregrine preceded the others into the dining room. They were followed by Lord Baltor and Cecily and the Nickleby's, with Mr. Smith bringing up the rear. When all were seated, only Mr. Smith was without a dinner companion, but Judith did not think that he minded in the least. He had tucked his napkin into his collar and rubbed his hands together over the first course of mince pies, barley soup, and a choice of vegetables. Her glance traveled about the table. Mrs. Nickleby was supplying her spouse with an opinion on the entrees of roast beef and the customary seasoned Christmas goose to which the gentleman was paying but half an ear, and no one else was giving even a semblance of polite attention.

Dusk fell at an early hour in the winter and the dining room had been lit with several branches of candles, which shed a soft glow over the faces of those present. Lord Baltor's and Cecily's shared glances and shining faces made the candlelight seem rather redundant, thought Judith. She could only feel misgivings about Cecily's obvious attraction to Lord Baltor. Not that his lordship was other than a pleasant young man, but this latest infatuation could only damage Cecily's case in Sir Peregrine's eyes.

"A penny for them."

Judith glanced around. Sir Peregrine's expression was quizzical. She shook her head and a fleeting smile crossed her face. "I was only reflecting on the caprices of human nature."

"Ah." Sir Peregrine's keen eyes immediately sought out his ward and Lord Baltor. He swung his glance back to the lovely lady at his side. And she was very lovely, he acknowledged silently, his eyes traveling slowly from her smooth-skinned face to the exquisite figure that was set off nicely by a close-cut velvet gown. He cocked his dark brow, his devastatingly keen gaze once more meeting her gray eyes. "Do I detect a hint of regret for opportunities lost, Judith?"

Judith had colored faintly under his scrutiny. Now she sucked her breath in startled surprise. Her eyes flashed at his audacity. "I am sure I do not know what you mean, Sir Peregrine," she said loftily.

Across the table, despite her absorption with Lord Baltor, Cecily had caught a portion of their quiet exchange. Her curiosity had been aroused earlier by Miss Grantham's obvious knowledge of Sir Peregrine's nature and now she had heard him address Miss Grantham by her given name. "Why, cousin, I did not know that you and Miss Grantham knew one another so well," she said in surprise.

Judith's eyes flew to meet Sir Peregrine's. He regarded her for an infinitesimal pause before he replied. "We are...old acquaintances." He gave his ward no chance to pursue the matter, as she seemed inclined to do, but at once asked Lord Baltor where he enjoyed shooting. Cecily's attention was immediately diverted as well as she listened spellbound to her new-found love expound on the types of sport one might find in his part of the country.

Judith was able to respond to a sally from Mr. Nickleby with all appearances of composure. She gradually relaxed as dinner progressed. It went far better than she had dared hope, there being no rash words between Sir Peregrine and Cecily and even few complaints from Mrs. Nickleby. Indeed, Cecily seemed in her best manners, thought Judith, approving of the subdued civility that the girl showed to her guardian and the rest. At least Sir Peregrine could not say that Cecily's head had been so turned by Lord Baltor's attentions that she had behaved in too forward a fashion.

When at last the ladies left the gentlemen to their wine and repaired to the drawing room, she was actually beginning to believe that the interview between Cecily and Sir Peregrine would also go off well.

"Miss Grantham, I do not feel at all the thing," said Cecily faintly.

Judith turned to look at her and she became instantly alarmed. The girl's eyes had become fever-bright and there were hectic patches of color in her cheeks. "My dear!" Judith laid a cool hand across Cecily's brow and her heart plunged. The girl was burning to the touch. "You must be gotten to bed instantly. I shall myself take you up to your room. Only wait one moment so that I may ring for something for the fever to be brought for you."

Mrs. Nickleby regarded Cecily's drooping figure in some alarm. She drew back her skirts from possible contamination. "Fever! I do hope that it is not catching. My dear Miss Brown, surely you could have shown more consideration for the rest of us and stayed up in your room if you were ill."

"I am sorry. I thought at first it was only my nerves that made me feel so peculiar," said Cecily. She sat down abruptly on a chair. Her flushed face had gone stark white.

Judith stared at Mrs. Nickleby with acute dislike. "Madam, I doubt that any fever would dare take residence in one of your constitution." Mrs. Nickleby opened and closed her mouth, astonished and confused by the biting set-down.

Judith tugged vigorously on the bell rope. The door to the drawing room was opened instantly by a footman. "John, Miss Brown has been taken ill. Ask Mrs. Wyssop to make up something for her fever. I shall myself help Miss Brown upstairs to her room." The footman bowed and hurried off on his errand.

Judith put her arm about Cecily's narrow shoulders and helped her rise from the chair. The girl swayed and Judith steadied her. "There you are, child. I shall not let you fall," she said gently.

Cecil threw a grateful glance up at her face. "You are unfailingly kind," she murmured. Judith admonished her not to speak but to concentrate on making her way up the stairs.

When Judith returned from settling Cecily comfortably in bed, she discovered that the gentlemen had taken up residence in the drawing room and that they had been informed by Mrs. Nickleby of Miss Brown's surprising collapse.

Sir Peregrine looked over at Judith, his visage a bit sardonic. "Protecting her to the last, are you?" he asked.

Judith's already frayed temper flared. She said coldly, "I do not know what you mean, Sir Peregrine." She turned her shoulder on him then and smiled encouragingly at Lord Baltor, who inquired rather anxiously of Miss Brown. "Miss Brown has apparently contracted a fever from becoming chilled yesterday, but I daresay that she will presently be much better."

Lord Baltor was struck with remorse. "It is my fault," he said hollowly.

"Indeed, it was, your lordship. A heavier-handed whipster I hope never to see! It is a wonder any of us escaped with nothing worse than a few bumps after being tossed hurley-burley into the snow," said Mrs. Nickleby with a decisive nod. She embarked on an involved recital of the accident to the mail coach and her thoughts on the matter.

Judith could not stifle an impatient exclamation. Sir Peregrine had the audacity to laugh. Pointedly ignoring him, Judith pinned a smile to her lips and set herself to endure what was left of what had been for the most part a trying day.

After a moment she heard someone whistling "Good King Wenceslaus". She turned her head in relief. "Mr. Smith, what a truly happy notion," she said.

The gentleman broke off in mid-note, disconcerted and faintly alarmed. But Judith was no longer looking at him. "Lord Baltor, let us do as you once suggested and lift the ceiling with a few Christmas carols." She seated herself at the pianoforte, the top of which was covered with an arrangement of laurel, bay, and rosemary that filled the air with spicy scent.

Lord Baltor was completely amenable to the suggestion, especially as it served to distract Mrs. Nickleby from her droning recital. "I am at your service, Miss Grantham," he said, positioning himself behind her shoulder.

A carol was quickly agreed upon and they lifted their voices in song. Sir Peregrine came to lean against the pianoforte and added a pleasant baritone. After a small hesitation, the remaining three joined in the singing. When it was done, Judith began playing another familiar old tune and this time the caroling was more resonant.

An hour had passed in the pleasant exercise when the butler entered the drawing room with a long taper. With some ceremony he lighted the kissing-bough candles, which had been lit for the first time on Christmas Eve and would be again each night of the twelve days of Christmas. As each wick caught, the appearance of the yellow flame was greeted with claps and good humor.

The company broke up soon afterward and good nights were exchanged. With a quiet request, Sir Peregrine delayed Judith's exit from the drawing room and he closed the door behind the others. Judith raised her brows in inquiry. She was astonished and obscurely pleased that Sir Peregrine's expression was exceptionally friendly. She thought that her own expression must reflect the same amicability that had been induced in them all by the caroling.

Sir Peregrine advanced toward her. "I wished to apologize for my manners earlier in the evening. It was ill-conceived of me to accuse you of spiriting away Cecily under pretense of malaise," he said.

Judith was still affected by the surprising pleasantness of the evening and she discovered that his apology put her in complete charity with him. "I have quite forgotten it," she said with her easy smile.

Sir Peregrine carried her hand to his lips. "You are gracious, Judith." He retained hold of her fingers. There was a decided twinkle in his extraordinary blue eyes. "You do realize that we are standing beneath the kissing bough."

Judith cast a disconcerted look up at the crown-shaped kissing bough and the mistletoe suspended from its center. She laughed. "So we are. Rest easy, sir. I do not subscribe to all of the Christmas traditions," she said reassuringly.

Sir Peregrine smiled. "But I do." He took her into his arms and kissed her slowly and thoroughly. Judith's thoughts tilted and tumbled into confusion.

Sir Peregrine released her. There was a curious expression in his eyes. "Merry Christmas, Judith," he said softly, and he left the drawing room.

Judith remained standing where he had left her for several seconds before she left the drawing room and made her way upstairs to her bedroom.

Chapter Eight

The two days following were marked by weak sunshine and the rising hopes of various members of the household that the snow had at last run its course. When the man who regularly delivered meat from the village butcher appeared at the servants' entrance, it was felt that Elmswood Hall would soon be back to normal. "That nosey-body is as good as gone," said Cook with satisfaction, and she began to plan a special menu to celebrate the happy event.

Miss Grantham would willingly have echoed her cook's sentiments. She heard the announcement about the weather with welcome relief, Withers having chosen to deliver it himself to the entire company when they were assembled for luncheon. "That is wonderful, indeed." She turned an inquiring gaze in the direction of her guests, her winged brows lifted. "Perhaps I may send a message to the posting house?"

"That would be fine for Mrs. Nickleby and myself. We should be getting on with our visit to our boy," said Mr. Nickleby. He tucked in the last bite of a meat pie. After eyeing the port wine trifle on the sideboard for a moment, he regretfully decided against it. He had eaten well and he did not think that he could swallow another mouthful.

Mrs. Nickleby's lips opened as she prepared herself to deliver a comment. Ruthlessly, Judith passed over her to address Mr. Smith. "And you, sir?" she asked, her smile appearing again.

Compared to the Nicklebys, Mr. Smith had been a paragon of a guest even though more than once his roaming about the house had served to give a fright to the maids when they had come upon him in unexpected places. She herself had discovered him again in the library and she had felt an initial surprise, for she had not thought he looked the sort who would enjoy books. But she had reminded herself that appearances could be deceiving. Thereafter she had made a point of commenting on some story or other that she had found of interest and Mr. Smith had seemed to appreciate her efforts because his eyes had crinkled up with a quiet humor that she had found endearing.

"Aye, miss. And I will be thanking you kindly," said Mr. Smith.

Judith nodded, appreciating his quiet manners – quite unlike some she could think of, who had not once uttered a gracious word, she thought. She turned her gaze on Lord Baltor, who was looking unhappy. "Why, is there something wrong, my lord?"

Lord Baltor hesitated a moment, vacillating. At last he took his courage in his hands. "The thing of it, Miss Grantham, is that I do not feel that I can take my leave just yet. I mean to say, it was my doing that caused Miss Brown to fall ill. I would not feel right to leave Elmswood without knowing- "

"You refine too much on it, Baltor," said Sir Peregrine impatiently.

Judith glanced at Sir Peregrine. She smiled warmly at Lord Baltor. "Your sentiments do you credit, my lord. Certainly, you may remain at Elmswood for as long as you would like. However, I do not wish you to sacrifice your time with your aunt. Did you not say previously that you were on your way to visit with her?"

"Oh, but she has not notion that I was coming. It was to be a surprise, so I daresay that a day or two more will make little difference," said Lord Baltor ingenuously.

"Quite," said Judith, not daring to glance at Sir Peregrine. She could sense that he was deriving much the same amusement as she was from Lord Baltor's artlessness. It was passing strange that she and Sir Peregrine could be so alike in some ways and yet set one another's backs up so readily, she thought. "Well, that is settled. I think that we shall all be glad to get on with our individual plans for the holiday, though I must say it has been quite an experience to have all of you here at

Elmswood. I do not think that I shall ever quite forget it," she said with an encompassing smile.

"Quite," murmured Sir Peregrine.

Judith ignored the thread of irony in his voice. She glanced at him in a determinedly friendly fashion. "Sir Peregrine, I know that you in particular have chafed at your enforced stay at Elmswood. But like Lord Baltor, I assure you of continued hospitality until Miss Brown is well enough to travel. Perhaps you would like to visit with your ward later today? Though I have not talked to Cecily, I think that a visit from you might underscore your concern for her well-being."

Her suggestion was couched with all the trappings of the solicitude of the polite hostess, but the gentleman to whom she addressed it was well able to gather a more pointed meaning to it. It was but another skirmish line in their ongoing battle.

"An excellent suggestion, Miss Grantham," said Sir Peregrine in appreciation. "I shall certainly do so." He smiled at her and he was surprised by the answering spark of merriment in her eyes. He realized that she also derived a certain enjoyment from the repartee between them. They had scarcely spoken more than a few sentences to each other in five years and it seemed that they were equally determined to make up for that oversight.

In particular, he recalled how right she had felt in his arms under the kissing bough. He could not for the life of him see where that could possibly lead since the past still hung there, unalterable and unpalatable. At the thought, his smile faded and a distinct chill entered his eyes. Luncheon was done with for all intents and purposes and he excused himself to the company.

Judith had seen the instant that Sir Peregrine's expression changed. His manner had gone cold of a sudden and the warmth in his eyes had become shuttered. It unsettled her. She had assumed after he had kissed her that their differences were on the way to being mended. However, she was not particularly sorry when he left the dining room.

She thought that if there was anything that she was sorry for, it was that Sir Peregrine would be remaining at Elmswood yet a while. His uncertain moods made the atmosphere distinctly uncomfortable.

That afternoon, shortly before the dinner hour, a commotion was raised above-stairs in a flurry of furious voices. Judith, who had been reading in the library, left her book in the chair and hurried out into the entry hall. The altercation was rapidly becoming louder and attracted the notice of all within earshot.

Sir Peregrine and Lord Baltor emerged from the billiards room, Sir Peregrine exclaiming, "What the devil?"

The footmen and a maid or two left their various tasks to step into the entry hall and Mr. Smith appeared from somewhere. They all stood in the hall, their faces raised in the direction of the balcony where the ruckus was originating.

Mrs. Nickleby hove into sight and marched down the stairs in full sail, her high accusing voice rising above the scared protestations of a slight maid, hauled along by Mr. Nickleby, who recommended the girl to keep her mouth closed or she would accuse herself all the deeper.

Mrs. Nickleby spied her hostess below. She seemed to swell. "Miss Grantham! I do not know what kind of household you find acceptable, but believe me, I would be ashamed to employ such persons as this wanton *thief!* A fine thing! As your guest, I expected much better. Indeed, I did, ma'am!" The Nicklebys and their captive came swiftly down the stairs, Mrs. Nickleby never letting up in her loud diatribe. Mr. Nickleby punctuated his wife's unrelenting scold by nods and occasional utterances of agreement.

Judith raised her voice. "Mrs. Nickleby! Pray calm yourself, madam. I cannot make any sense of this at all." She might as well have tried to quell a storm.

Sir Peregrine was not so helpless. He said in his direct way, "Mr. Nickleby, if you do not have the decency to shut your wife up, then I shall be forced to do so." His level gaze was hard.

Mr. Nickleby apparently took him at his word. He let go of the maid and shook his wife's arm. The maid scuttled quickly behind Withers, who had come into the hall, and peeped fearfully out around him at the Nicklebys. "That's enough now, pet. We have Miss Grantham's undivided attention, of a certainty."

"So I should hope!" exclaimed Mrs. Nickleby. She pointed a shaking finger at the maid, who squeaked in fright. "That is the one! That is the thief. She denies it, but she has taken my rubies!"

"I never, Miss Grantham! I couldn't have done such a thing," said the maid, practically in tears.

"Miss Grantham, I assure you that no one under my command is capable of what this...lady suggests," said Withers, not demeaning himself by even so much as a glance in Mrs. Nickleby's direction.

Judith nodded her awareness of the butler's patent outrage. "Mrs. Nickleby, perhaps if you could tell me why you believe your rubies have been stolen, then perhaps we may come to some sort of conclusion," she said calmly.

"My rubies are missing and that little hussy stole them," said Mrs. Nickleby. "All that talk of replacing a button on my cloak! Phah! She was but learning where my jewel case was kept, weren't you, missy?"

Pandemonium broke loose. The maid squeaked her innocence. Withers raised his voice, his indignation plain. "Miss Grantham, I must take leave to observe-" Mrs. Nickleby roared her disbelief, reiterating her accusations.

"That is quite enough!" Judith's voice cracked through the air. Instantly the hall fell quiet, various pairs of eyes fixing on her face with surprise or approval, depending upon their owners.

"Good girl," murmured Sir Peregrine under his breath. He entirely approved of the tide of rose in Miss Grantham's face and the manner in which her gray eyes flashed.

Judith looked at Mr. Nickleby and said coldly, "Since your wife appears quite incapable of expressing herself with any degree of control, I should like to hear the tale from you. If you please, Mr. Nickleby!"

Mr. Nickleby was nothing loath. "It is as my good wife has been saying, Miss Grantham. The ruby necklace and earrings are gone, as well as the ring, and a pretty penny I paid for them, too. That maid there has been serving Mrs. Nickleby since we come. She had the opportunity. And it did seem suspicious at the time that she claimed to want to replace a button on Mrs. Nickleby's cloak without being told. Why, I ask you, what servant offers to do the extra thing? No, as I told Mrs. Nickleby, that maid has done the deed. She was but throwing dust in our eyes, being so helpful."

"On the contrary. Those I employ anticipate the needs of myself and of my guests. If that is not what you are used to, I am sorry for it; but certainly, that does not give you leave to wantonly accuse any member of my staff of thievery or falsehood," said Judith with distaste. "If your rubies are missing as you say, they have probably only been misplaced and will certainly turn up in time."

"Did I not tell you, Mr. Nickleby? Did I not say that the servant was but an extension of the mistress's own lax nature? I would not be a bit surprised to learn that Miss Grantham is every bit as larcenous as that wretched maid!" exclaimed Mrs. Nickleby.

There were several indrawn breaths among the fascinated audience and all eyes flew to Judith's face. She stood quite still, her face white and expressionless. Only her glittering eyes, which had paled almost to silver, gave away her cold rage. "Mr. Nickleby, your wife has worn out my hospitality. I shall appreciate your departure within a quarter hour. A carriage will be readied immediately to carry you to the posting house."

Mr. Nickleby found himself making a bow and he straightened up hastily, annoyed with himself that he had been intimidated by Miss

Grantham's lofty air. "There is still the question of my good wife's jewels, Miss Grantham."

Judith looked at the gentleman for such a long moment that he became restive. She said thinly, "I am so anxious to have you out of my home that I shall happily pay whatever the wretched stones are worth."

"There! If that is not an admission of guilt, I have never heard one," said Mrs. Nickleby. "Tell her that I shall have my rubies, Mr. Nickleby."

Mr. Nickleby paid his spouse no attention. A shrewd look had entered his eyes. "The stones came dear enough, but I shall be satisfied with five hundred pounds for the set."

Sir Peregrine gave a short, sharp laugh. "My dear sir, you shall catch cold at this game. I shall not stand by tamely and allow Miss Grantham to be shamelessly fleeced. You'll take a hundred pounds and count yourself fortunate that I do not throw you and your wife out on your collective ears."

Mr. Nickleby nodded. "Done, sir." Mrs. Nickleby was outraged, and made her feelings known in no uncertain terms.

Judith thought she must get away from the awful woman or she would not be able to retain control over her temper. She turned on her heel and walked swiftly toward the stairs.

"But what of my rubies?" shrilled Mrs. Nickleby, surging after her.

Judith paused, her hand on the balustrade, and looked down at her from the advantage of the first step. "My dear madam, you are fortunate that one of my extremely larcenous nature does not strip you of the petticoats that you stand in!" she uttered. Without a backward glance she went swiftly up the stairs.

Chapter Nine

Judith took refuge in her private sitting room, done in pale lime silk and cherry wood that gave it a warm effect. She paced about the pretty room, giving full rein to her fury for several minutes.

A servant timidly knocked to inquire if she would be joining the gentlemen downstairs for dinner or if she wished to be served dinner in her room, to both of which she gave an emphatic negative but added that she would like tea. By the time that the servant brought in the tea and a selection of biscuits, she had calmed considerably and she was even able to swallow a few bits of biscuit.

When her maid quietly entered to relay a request from Sir Peregrine that he be allowed to wait on her, Judith was able to view the prospect of once more playing hostess with equanimity. Judith indicated that she would see him and seated herself in front of the fire.

When Sir Peregrine strolled into the sitting room, he was struck immediately by her air of unruffled composure. He said humorously, "My word, I thought to find you rending the draperies at least."

Judith laughed at such a fitting description of her recent state. "I hope that I am too old for such dramatics, though I will admit to a strong desire to strangle a certain vulgar female."

"If I had known, I most certainly would have delayed the Nicklebys' departure for such an admirable inclination. But unfortunately, I myself saw them off more than an hour past," said Sir Peregrine. He suddenly grinned at her. "You were magnificent, Judith."

Judith flushed and pressed her palms against the heat of her cheeks. "Oh dear! My wretched temper. I so very nearly disgraced myself."

"True, but in such a noble cause. However, Mr. Smith was apparently so overawed that he preferred to share a carriage with a hysterical Mrs. Nickleby and her increasingly short-tempered spouse rather than outstay his own welcome," said Sir Peregrine.

Judith felt thoroughly ashamed of herself. "That poor unassuming little man. I grew rather fond of him." She gestured at the small table beside her chair, upon which sat the teapot. "I usually have tea at this hour, as you see. Pray won't you join me, Sir Peregrine?"

"Thank you, I should like that, I think," said Sir Peregrine. He seated himself opposite and idly watched as she poured. He declined sugar or milk and took the cup from her hand. "By the by, I have visited Cecily. I do not think that I shall tear her from Elmswood just yet. She appears on the mend, but I shall not risk bringing on a relapse of her fever by traveling in this weather."

"I am happy to hear that your good sense prevails," said Judith with a touch of soft irony.

Sir Peregrine's eyes lighted with laughter even as he acknowledged her thrust. "I am not so lost to a proper sense of my responsibilities as to risk my ward's health, whatever thoughts you may have had on the matter."

"Why, sir, I would not dream of interfering," said Judith with bland innocence.

"Quite," said Sir Peregrine dryly. "I noticed, however, that Cecily is becoming restless at her enforced inactivity and I have given permission for Lord Baltor to visit with her. He seems willing enough to wait on her, while I harbor no such inclinations. You will say next that I am shirking my duty not to dance to whatever tune Cecily wishes to pipe."

"Not that, no," said Judith instantly. "But do you think it wise to throw Cecily and Lord Baltor together in such a fashion? They were so taken with one another, after all."

Sir Peregrine brushed such considerations aside. "Cecily will be madly in love with the fellow for six weeks and then she will quite literally forget his lordship's name. Believe me, I have seen the pattern before. She'll take no hurt from proximity with Lord Baltor. As for his lordship, one always makes a recovery from one's first calf love."

"You are cynical, sir," said Judith, smiling at him over the rim of her cup. Sir Peregrine returned her smile and bowed from the waist in acknowledgement of her observation. She was aware that several seconds had ticked by and she marveled at the usual ease of their companionship. She spoke her thoughts. "Do you know, I believe this is the first time that we have managed a civil conversation of any length between us? It is...pleasant."

"We did not often use our times together to such advantage," said Sir Peregrine in agreement.

"No. We were engaged more in seeking out one another's weaknesses. Those are not particularly good memories," said Judith quietly, her eyes contemplating the fire.

"It is odd, but I do recall a few good memories," said Sir Peregrine softly.

Judith's eyes flew to his and what she saw in his expression made the color rise in her face. "Perhaps there were some," she acknowledged. "But the quarrels between us overwhelmed any sort of lasting affection." She was silent a moment before she summoned up a smile. "Actually, I am surprised to feel so much in charity with you. I do not know what has come over us. We have not ripped up one another for the better part of two days."

Sir Peregrine studied her face. "I suppose that we have become infected by the yuletide season."

"Yes, I suppose that must be it," said Judith. She felt distinct dissatisfaction that he offered such a simple explanation. It had not been the Christmas spirit that had set her pulses racing when he kissed her. But certainly, she could not have expected an acknowledgement of anything more from him.

A knock at the sitting room door heralded the entrance of Withers. Judith looked inquiringly at the butler. "Yes, Withers, what is it?"

Withers' usual expressionless countenance appeared troubled. "Miss, I have come with rather singular tidings," he said. He advanced toward her and held out his hand. In his palm was a gold band set with a large ruby.

Judith instantly recognized Mrs. Nickleby's lost ruby ring. "My word! Wherever was it found?" she asked, taking it between her fingers. The ruby flashed in the light.

"It was found in Mr. Smith's room, together with this note," said Withers. He handed a twist of paper to her.

Judith smoothed open the note. It took but a moment to scan it. Then she went into a peal of laughter. Sir Peregrine instantly demanded to be let in on the joke and she thrust the note at him. "Here, sir! Read it for yourself! I was never more amused in my life," she gasped.

Reading the note, Sir Peregrine started to laugh as well. "Our John Smith seems to have been a cunning devil. Who could have guessed that he was a thief? And an honorable one at that."

"Indeed, and I had thought that he was reading on those occasions that I found him in the library. I never dreamed that he was squirreling away odd bits of silver and Mrs. Nickleby's jewelry!" said Judith, still chuckling. She looked up at the faintly disapproving expression on Withers' face. "Come, Withers, surely you must see the humor. It is not every day that a thief leaves a token of his appreciation for the hospitality of Elmswood!" As she spoke, she held up the ruby ring.

"The hospitality was not all that John Smith admired, Miss Grantham. He appeared quite impressed when you dealt so summarily with Mrs. Nickleby. I suspect that was what persuaded him to leave your silver spoons in the library," said Sir Peregrine.

"I suppose that I must be flattered," said Judith, laughing again.

"A most singular gentleman, indeed. I shall go at once to the library and retrieve the silver," said Withers repressively. He nodded at the ring. "Shall I take custody of that object, ma'am?"

"Pray do so," said Judith promptly. She handed over the ring. She shook her head as the butler left the sitting room. "I fear that it will be some time before Withers can look on this with any degree of humor. He has taken it as a personal failing that he was not able to see through Mr. Smith's mild demeanor."

Her quiet words seemed to trigger a parallel of recognition in her companion. "We all fail to correctly divine an individual's character on occasion," said Sir Peregrine, all levity gone from his expression.

Judith stared at him, her heart beginning to sink. The truce between them was obviously over. "Quite true. I think we may agree on that point, Perry," she said coolly.

He smiled, though no amusement appeared in his eyes. "We seem to have come to another Rubicon, Judith. Being in your company these past days has forced me to acknowledge a desire to understand what happened between us. I do not think that I shall let you go until we have hammered it out."

Judith gave the faintest of laughs. The ironic expression in her eyes was reflected in her voice. "It does seem the perfect opportunity, does it not? Perhaps this time we may even manage to preserve a semblance of civility."

"The rules are established, then. Civility and frankness are the only limits. And as a gentleman, I must bow to your prerogative to begin," said Sir Peregrine with a wolfish grin.

Judith stopped herself from delivering a withering set-down. It would hardly forward relations if she were to immediately set up his back, and quite suddenly she wished very much to be able to hold this frightening conversation.

Quite frightening, she thought, aware of her dry throat and the tenseness of her shoulders. But she would not give way to it, as she had before. There was deeply buried pain within her that had never quite healed. She knew now it never would unless she went through this confrontation.

A long silence fell while Judith thought over and rejected a dozen questions. There was one that had always stayed at the forefront of her mind, but she did not have quite the courage to ask it. Despising herself for a coward, she said, "I have found certain contentment in my life. I have always wondered whether you did as well."

Sir Peregrine gave a short laugh. His piercing eyes derided her timid start. "I suppose one may say so. I do not lack for friends, if that is what you mean."

Judith bit her lip. She felt ready to sink, but from somewhere she found the courage to continue the dangerous game. "Have you – have you a female companion?" she asked hesitantly.

He was silent a moment. "No. I am not entangled in any sort of relationship. But surely you know that?"

She shook her head. "No one ever speaks of you to me, you see." She gestured helplessly. "It was as though there was always a determination to shelter me from anything that might cause me unpleasantness. Or more likely, to ward off any possibility of my making an uncomfortable scene if I were to learn anything I did not quite like."

Sir Peregrine regarded her steadily. "Would you have? Made a scene, I mean."

Judith laughed, though a bit shakily. "Oh, I don't know. Perhaps early on, but at this point it hardly matters, does it? We have grown inured to one another's existence and in the last few days we have proven that we are even able to be civil toward one another. That in itself is rather refreshing, do you not think?"

"I think that we were both fools," said Sir Peregrine forcibly.

Judith looked over at him in astonishment.

He got swiftly to his feet and turned to stare into the fire, presenting his hard profile to her. "Do not look at me like that, Judith.

You do not know what your eyes say to me." He glanced around at her then and his mouth curved into a rueful smile. "You always had the most bewitching eyes; did I ever tell you?"

Judith clasped her fingers tightly together. She felt as though she was about to suffocate. "No, I do not think so. But then there was not much time for such words."

Sir Peregrine gave a bark of laughter. "That is surely an understatement, my girl! We fought nearly every moment that we were ever together, which was not often since we were surrounded by a constant crowd of the curious. It was a ridiculous courtship. In public we were the epitome of polite breeding, smiling and gracious to every personage who wished to congratulate us on what a splendid match we were making. It makes me ill now to recall how I allowed myself, and you, to go through that rot, when all I wanted was to speak to you alone and to make love you. My God, Judith, why did you jilt me?"

Color flamed in her cheeks. She stared at her hands, clasped tightly in her lap. Her voice came low and intense. "I discovered that you were bought for me."

Sir Peregrine swung around. "What the devil are you talking about?" he snapped.

Chapter Ten

There was a commotion at the door and it was thrust open. Cecily's voice sounded a determined note. "I do not care! I shall speak to him at once, Arthur!" She came into the sitting room on the tail of her words. Lord Baltor was close on her heels, his countenance perturbed.

Cecily stopped when she saw Miss Grantham's expressionless face and her guardian's unfriendly gaze. She raised her delectably pointed chin. "Forgive my intrusion, Miss Grantham. But I was told that I would find my cousin with you and I must speak to him at once."

"Of course, Cecily. Pray join us, and you also, my lord," said Judith, her experience as a hostess granting her the poise she required to form a gracious reply. Her lips felt stiff as she smiled. She gestured to the settee situated near the fireplace.

Cecily shook her head. "We shall stay but a moment, I think. At least-" As her eyes went to Sir Peregrine's grim expression, her voice faltered slightly. She felt Lord Baltor's fingers on her elbow and the contact gave her courage. "Sir Peregrine, I have come to inform you that I have engaged myself to Lord Baltor. I shall therefore refuse to consider the suit of the gentleman whom you chose for me. I hope that this does not come as too great a shock to you and that you will grant us your blessing," she said in formal tones.

"You shall catch cold waiting for it," said Sir Peregrine pithily. He looked at Lord Baltor with something akin to impatience. "Come, Baltor, you do not truly wish to tie yourself to my flighty ward. She tumbles in and out of love with such regularity that I have become resigned to it. Believe me, you would do better to wait on a more steadfast maiden."

"I am aware of Cecily – Miss Brown's – past, sir. She has informed me of it herself, which but adds to my admiration," said Lord Baltor.

"I have not the stomach for this," muttered Sir Peregrine. He met Judith's gaze for a second only, because she at once turned her head away, but he was quite able to read the censure in her eyes. It gave him pause.

"Perry, I know that I have given you cause to mistrust my steadiness. So, I have thought up a compromise, if you should like it," said Cecily. She clasped her hands in front of her. "I have discussed the matter with Arthur and he has agreed that my plan is reasonable."

Sir Peregrine threw a sardonic look at Lord Baltor, who met his gaze unflinchingly even though a flush rose in his boyish face. "I see. Pray continue, Cecily. I cannot deny you a hearing, I suppose."

Cecily drew a breath. "I am under age, of course, so you have the right to squelch any union that I may wish until I attain my majority. I know that I have at last truly fallen in love, but I realize that I must prove that to you. So, I propose that an informal understanding be recognized between myself and Lord Baltor. In the meantime, I should like to be brought out in London so that I may be exposed to positively scores of gentlemen. If I do not change my allegiance from Lord Baltor to another in the year before my majority is up, you will agree to a formal announcement of our engagement to be inserted in the *Gazette*."

There was a short silence during which Sir Peregrine studied his ward with an unreadable expression. He said finally, "You have at last succeeded in surprising me, Cecily. It seems that you have learned a bit of common sense. Your stay at Elmswood seems to have been to your advantage." He did not glance toward Judith, but he sensed her start of astonishment.

Cecily flushed with the beginnings of excitement. "Then you do agree to my compromise?"

"I think that I do," said Sir Peregrine. He glanced at Lord Baltor. "And now, my lord, you may escort my ward back to her parlor. She appears ready to faint at my easy acquiescence."

The young couple extricated themselves from the sitting room with several exclamations of thanks. When the door was closed behind them, Judith glanced at Sir Peregrine with a faint smile. "I am glad for Cecily."

"At this moment I care not one jot about my ward's future," said Sir Peregrine. He stared frowningly at Judith. "I believe that we left off with a positively idiotic statement regarding my motives for offering for you. Pray enlighten me further, Miss Grantham!"

Judith stiffened and something flashed in her expression. Her eyes challenged him, daring him to deny her accusation. "You were my father's choice. After we became engaged, he congratulated himself for having struck a bargain with you, though it had cost him what he termed a tidy little sum!"

Old anger had laced her tumble of words, but now she sighed. She passed hand over her eyes. "He told me that I should be a grateful daughter because he had found such a splendid match for me. I knew in that instant I could never be happy with you."

Her eyes were shadowed when she looked at him. "I had thought you cared for me a little. It was unbearable that you had offered for me for quite different reasons. Oh, I know that marriages are still arranged and that bride's money changes hands, but I was a naïve and romantic young girl and that was not what I wanted for myself."

Sir Peregrine had been riveted by her account. He understood now why a few days previously she had been so hostile when he had mentioned bribing away one of Cecily's undesirable suitors. He expelled a breath. "That is when you decided to reject my suit, then."

Judith shook her head. "I did not know what to do."

"Judith, why did you not come to me? I would have told you the truth," said Sir Peregrine quietly.

"What was the truth, Perry?" she asked.

He felt bitterness spark to life, but after an instant he thrust it aside. Pride had once led him to walk away without demanding an explanation. He would not allow himself to make that same mistake again. He must keep his own end of the bargain as well as she had. "Your father approached me to arrange a match between us. I was entirely taken aback by such an arrangement being offered in this day and age. Looking back on it, I think that he must have thought my hesitation due to lack of monetary incentive. That was when he offered that damnable 'tidy little sum.'"

Sir Peregrine gave a fleeting half-smile as his eyes studied Judith's tight expression. He continued quietly, "But once I had a moment to think about you, I discovered that your father had merely anticipated my own unformed desires. I had already met you and become intrigued by you. The money that your father spoke about meant nothing to me. I was ready to set it immediately in trust for you to use as you wished. I hoped that you would pass it on to any children that we might have."

Judith's expression had altered and become vulnerable as he spoke. The last completely overset her. She covered her face with her hands. "Dear God, how could I have been so wrong?" she whispered.

"Judith." Sir Peregrine knelt beside her chair and gently pulled her hands down, to hold both clasped between his own fingers. "My very dear Judith, why did you never tell me? We could have saved one another so much anger and bitterness."

Judith's smile wavered. "You have said it yourself, Perry. We were not given much time to learn about one another. Whenever we were private, we either fought or you kissed me. I could not keep a single coherent thought in my head."

A light entered Sir Peregrine's blue eyes. "That is most interesting, Miss Grantham." He slowly leaned closer.

Judith watched him come, mesmerized. As his lips brushed hers, her lashes fluttered down. His mouth tasted wonderful and the kiss was heady as wine. The familiar swirl of melting feeling began to engulf her.

Realizing it, Judith broke away. She pulled free her hands and pushed against his broad shoulders. "Perry, do not," she whispered. For several seconds she was afraid that he would reject her plea. He was still so close that she could feel the warmth of his breath on her face. But then he sighed and eased away from her.

"You are right, Judith. We have still too much that lies between us," said Sir Peregrine. He rose to his feet and moved deliberately to stand at the mantel so that there was distance between them. "You have said that it was the discovery that your father had offered money to me that decided you against my suit. But I seem to recall quite a different explanation that you gave to me. It sounded a pack of nonsense designed to insult me. But what so deeply enraged me, and what I have carried from that day to this, was your assertion that you feared me."

Judith sighed and shook her head. "I tried to explain feelings that I did not myself understand. What I did understand was that I was frightened. You see, I did not really know you and what my father said had shaken my faith in what I thought I knew. I was frightened and I had no one to ask for counsel. All my life I had never been able to withstand my father's will on any occasion, accepting his decisions for my future even when I was caused unhappiness. But my marriage to you- "

She looked at Sir Peregrine somberly. "I would be giving my life into what had become the hands of a complete stranger. I tried to talk to my father, but he paid me not the least heed. He patted me on the head and recommended that I turn my thoughts to my trousseau. My father wished our marriage to take place just as he had planned, but as the date approached my fear of the unknown became stronger than my awe of him. I did not consult with my father before I saw you that day. He was...disappointed." She could not keep the hurt out of her voice.

She had been a frightened young girl sorely in need of support and comfort, but that was not what she had received.

When Sir Peregrine recalled that her father had been a burly gentleman possessed of s supreme confidence in his own opinion, he thought that Judith had surely understated the man's reaction. All these years he had harbored an erroneous conclusion. His estimation of her mettle had been sadly wanting, he thought. "I know that your father must have made your life very difficult," he said quietly.

Judith brushed it aside. "It is unimportant now." She smiled at him wearily. "You must think me a perfect fool, I know."

Sir Peregrine shook his head. "On the contrary. That is what I thought then, but now I can only salute your courage. You flew in the face of all that you were taught to revere in order to preserve your integrity. I, on the other hand, behaved with as little common sense as I have credited Cecily with. I was so blinded by my own pride and anger that I scarcely listened to what you tried so inexpertly to convey to me."

The emotional intensity of the past several minutes was proving to be a terrible strain. Judith felt that she simply had to place the situation back into proper perspective or she feared that she would burst into tears. "I shall ring for sackcloth and ashes if you wish."

For an instant he was completely taken aback. Then he grinned and there was fondness in his eyes as he looked at her. "You are the most obliging hostess of my acquaintance, I must say. Thank you, but I believe that I will do very well without." He straightened up from his leaning posture against the mantel. Lifting her hand, he carried it to his lips. "Good night, Miss Grantham."

Judith smiled up at him tremulously. "Good night, Sir Peregrine." She watched him go to the sitting room door. She had never asked him whether he still loved her, she thought. But perhaps it was just as well. She was not certain that she really wished to hear the answer.

Sir Peregrine opened the door, but he did not go through immediately. Judith stood up. She felt that she had never been more tired in her life. It was difficult to recall that the tail end of the yuletide holidays were normally the quietest days of the year for her. "Was there anything else, Sir Peregrine?" she asked.

"I do not think that I can allow you to dwindle into an old maid," he said reflectively.

Judith gasped in outrage, quick color flying into her face. "I beg your pardon!"

Sir Peregrine came toward her, his expression unreadable. When he was within touching distance of her, he said, "I have been haunted these past five years, I thought by my hatred for what you had done. But that was merely hiding the truth from myself. Judith, when I think of the years stretching ahead without you beside me, I find it a very dull and empty vision. I fear that I am still very much in love with you."

Her indignation at his outrageous announcement faded away. On a sigh, Judith walked into his arms, which folded tight about her. She caught hold of his lapel. "That is just what I wished to hear, my old and enduring love."

Sir Peregrine put a hand under her chin and raised her face. His bright, piercing eyes laughed at her. "I mean to kiss you, you know."

"Pray do so," breathed Judith.

He took her at her word.

Other Books by Gayle Buck
The Righteous Rakehell Mutual Consent
Willowswood Match The Demon Rake
Love's Masquerade The Fleeing Heiress
Cassandra's Deception Belle's Beau
Magnificent Match Honor Beseiged
Lady Althea's Bargain Love For Lucinda
Frederica's Folly Chester Charade
Cupid's Choice Lord Darlington's Darling
A Chance Encounter The Waltzing Widow
Tempting Sarah Lord John's Lady
Lord Rathbone's Flirt The Desperate Viscount
Hearts Betrayed The Hidden Heart
Miss Dower's Paragon Lady Cecily's Scheme
<u>Regency Tales</u>
Old Acquaintances The Holybrooke Curse
Christmas Cheer Season of Joy
Alegria Navidena
<u>Regency Duets</u>
Cassandra's Deception & Belle's Beau
The Hidden Heart & The Desperate Viscount
Chester Charade & The Fleeing Heiress
The Waltzing Widow & Hearts Betrayed
Lord John's Lady & The Magnificent Match
The Holybrooke Curse & Cupid's Choice
Regency Tales: Christmas Collection

Don't miss out!

Visit the website below and you can sign up to receive emails whenever Gayle Buck publishes a new book. There's no charge and no obligation.

https://books2read.com/r/B-A-AISJ-ZGIDB

Also by Gayle Buck

Tempting Sarah
The Waltzing Widow
The Holybrooke Curse
Season of Joy
Hearts Betrayed
Chistmas Cheer
Old Acquaintances
Mutual Consent
The Chester Charade
The Desperate Viscount
Lady Althea's Bargain
Fredericka's Folly
Love for Lucinda
Lord Darlington's Darling
The Demon Rake
Lord Rathbone's Flirt
Miss Dower's Paragon
Belle's Beau
Cassandra's Deception
Love's Masquerade
The Righteous Rakehell
A Magnificent Match
The Hidden Heart
Willowswood Match
A Chance Encounter

The Fleeing Heiress
Lady Cecily's Scheme
Cupid's Choice
Lord John's Lady
Honor Besieged